### She Confessed Her Mischief and Incurred His Ire

"In London, trapping a husband is the latest sport," Jason assured her.

"Are you so against marriage, then?"

"No, of course not. But I do not think a man should be pressured into it. Your brother and I arrived here with the specific object of avoiding marriage schemes . . . But I have lost another friend to marriage. I suppose I should be grateful that his marriage is of his own choosing and not a scheme thought up by his sister." When Jason turned to look at the young woman beside him, his glance sharpened. "You did not arrange this marriage also, did you?"

"Don't be ridiculous. You know the whole story."

"Then why do you look so guilty?"

"Because I had already decided to promote such a match, once Papa was settled."

Jason sprang to his feet, staring down at her accusingly. "I cannot believe it! How could you consider such a thing? And I suppose I was next on your list? Do you have another friend waiting to be paired off with me?"

Anger got the better of wisdom and Georgina spat back, "No, I would not offer such a miserable excuse for a husband to my worst enemy, much less a friend!"

# Sweet Remembrance

## Judy Christenberry

DIAMOND BOOKS, NEW YORK

SWEET REMEMBRANCE

A Diamond Book/published by arrangement with the author

PRINTING HISTORY
Diamond edition/February 1992

ISBN: 1-55773-663-4

Diamond Books are published by The Berkley Publishing Group,
200 Madison Avenue, New York, New York 10016.
The name "DIAMOND" and its logo are trademarks
belonging to Charter Communications, Inc.

PRINTED IN THE UNITED STATES OF AMERICA

10 9 8 7 6 5 4 3 2 1

# Sweet Remembrance

# Prologue

The two elegant young men lounging in leather armchairs in the corner of White's Reading Room had lapsed into silence. Finally, the blond, his well-defined features accented by dark brows, gave a lugubrious sigh.

"I am bored, Denbigh. I have been bored since our return from routing Boney, and I do not see any hope of escaping boredom in the future."

"Come now, Jason, it is not that bad. After all, you have Lady Briarly fairly panting to replace the lovely Marietta in your bed," Mr. Denbigh reminded his friend, the Earl of Chesterton. "Every buck in London envies you."

"Envies my fortune. It is the prospect of generous gifts that inspires Lady Briarly's ardor and Marietta's faithfulness, and well you know it."

Mr. Denbigh gave an amused chuckle, but he denied his friend's assessment. "Old Cruickshank has almost as much wealth as you, but I don't see either of the aforementioned ladies offering their charms at *his* door."

Jason smiled wryly at his companion. "I will not deny that. But it is my fortune that draws them most. You are accounted the more handsome of the two of us, Nathaniel, and you know Lady Briarly would choose me because of my wealth. Regretfully."

1

"You have no interest in the lady?" Mr. Denbigh asked, his eyebrows rising. Lady Briarly was one of society's Diamonds.

"No more than any other. In my youth, I might have enjoyed variety, but even that has palled."

"In my youth!" Mr. Denbigh exclaimed with a laugh. "I see no grey hairs on your head, man."

"They seldom show in blond hair," Lord Chesterton said solemnly.

"You are not serious?" Nathaniel Denbigh asked.

With another sigh, the earl shrugged his shoulders. "I do not know. Life seems uninteresting at present."

Mr. Denbigh sobered. Their friendship was of long standing, and he took his friend's lament seriously. "I think you are spoiled, Jason."

"I do not take your meaning."

"D'not grow haughty with me, my friend. And I do not mean anything insulting by my words. But you are surrounded by people dedicated to meeting your every need before you are even aware of it. How long has it been since you had to tend to your own needs?" Nathaniel asked.

"I don't recall hordes of servants following us about on the Continent." With a snort of laughter, the earl added, "Wellington wouldn't have stood for it."

"Exactly, old chap. You said you have been bored since your return from the campaign against Napoleon three years ago." With a grin, Nathaniel pressed home his point. "And that just happens to be the last time you were called upon to act for yourself."

Lord Chesterton's smokey grey eyes stared across the room, and his friend waited patiently for a response. When those eyes turned their gaze back to Mr. Denbigh, the earl said slowly, "Perhaps you are right, Nathaniel. I should have realized how stifled I am. Ever since I came into the title, I have been surrounded by servants and hangers-on." Before his companion could take offense, he added, "Excepting you, Nathaniel. You have cared nothing for my wealth."

Mr. Denbigh smiled with an endearing grin that lit up his handsome features. "Ah, there is a reason for my faithfulness. My auburn locks look so admirable next to your blond." With a quickness that had served him well on the Continent, Nathaniel dodged his friend's playful jab.

"Careful, Jason, or you will disturb the folds of your cravat and ruin your reputation as a dandy."

"And if you are not careful, Nathaniel, I will wreak vengeance on your face. You may be the more handsome, but Gentleman Jackson will proclaim me to be the one most handy with his fists."

"No contest, Jason," Nathaniel acknowledged gratefully, delighted to see a smile on his friend's face.

Lord Chesterton sobered as he returned to their discussion. "I think you have the right of it, Nathaniel, but what shall I do? I cannot renounce the title, and I am not fool enough to renounce the fortune. Where is the remedy?"

"Perhaps if you disappear for a few days and assume a different identity? You could—no! I have a splendid idea."

"Well, what is it, man?" Lord Chesterton demanded.

"You shall come home with me. Georgie has commanded my presence for the Christmas season. The town is thin of company anyhow. Come with me to Greenbriar Manor."

"Georgie? Little Georgie," Lord Chesterton said, savoring his words. "I had forgotten about Georgie. How is she, Nathaniel? Is she all grown up? Do you remember that summer?''

"How could I forget? We were constantly in difficulty with my father.'' The pair had spent their eighteenth summer at Greenbriar Manor. Though Lord Chesterton had inherited his title and estates the previous summer, after their last year at Eton the two young men had retired to Nathaniel's home.

An expression of lingering pleasure settled on Lord Chesterton's features. "Your father was amazingly tolerant. And he seemed to understand my need for someone to guide me. As I recall, your father even wrote me when we were on the Continent.'' A frown wiped away his pleasure. "I should have at least visited him upon our return, especially since your mother had passed away.''

"It was a difficult time for him, but I'm sure he understood.'' Nathaniel himself had an uneasy conscience. He had spent little enough time with his family in the past three years, but he had suffered a restlessness after his soldiering that was not appeased with country life.

"He was certainly kindness itself when I injured his favorite hunter.''

"It was an accident, and you were awash with remorse. There was no reason to berate you,'' Nathaniel assured him.

"Some men would have. And your mother never minded the mud we tramped into the house from the fields. However, she did object that we taught Georgie to swim,'' Jason remembered with a laugh. "She said she would never be able to turn her into a lady after we finished with her.''

"She made a rather good fisherman, too, did she not?" Nathaniel added, grinning.

"Little Georgie," Jason repeated. "What a sweet remembrance she is." There was silence as memories paraded themselves before the two men. "Do you think your father would object to my accompanying you?" Jason finally asked.

# Chapter One

"She will never believe me," Tabitha Twickenham said to her best friend.

"Of course she will, Tabby. Nathaniel is terribly handsome—and I am not saying that just because I am his sister. Anne will not be at all surprised to discover you topsy-turvy over him. And since she is your companion, she must chaperone you." Georgina Denbigh frowned as she considered the finer points of her plan.

Tabitha drew closer to the warmth of the fireplace in the Denbighs' parlor. "But what if your brother objects to having me swoon over him—even as a ruse. After all, I am not—not of the nobility." The young woman's pale cheeks flushed at her admission.

"But that is the beauty of the plan," Georgina said happily. "Your mother's family is perfectly acceptable and nothing is required of Nathaniel." She frowned a moment. "Perhaps Nathaniel won't even notice. After all, girls have been enamoured of him in the past, and he is a trifle self-absorbed. All we need is an excuse for you to visit often and bring Anne along."

"She enjoys visiting here, I know. I think she is already interested in your father, though she would never admit it." With a sigh, Tabitha added, "I will miss her quite dreadfully if we succeed in making a match between her and your father.''

Georgina patted her arm. "Do not be concerned, Tabby. Once we have settled Anne, we will look around for someone for you.''

"Oh, no!'' This time Tabby flushed scarlet. "I did not mean—that is, we both know I am a failure in the marriage stakes.''

Georgina ignored her friend's protests. "Watch your tongue! Anne would be appalled at your using such a vulgar term.'' When Tabitha looked guilt-stricken, Georgina added, "I was only teasing, Tabby. You must not be so timid. It was not your fault you didn't find a husband. You were so young and your father treated you unkindly.'' Georgina leaned away from her friend and assessed her attributes.

In truth, her friend's pale blond hair, almost silver in color, and her pink complexion often drew many admiring looks, but Tabitha's shyness prevented her from noticing the attention. When they attended the local assembly balls, she often stared at the floor in fright. Georgina hoped Tabitha could find the courage to pull this ruse off. Tabitha's father had successfully quashed any signs of determination in his daughter many times in the past.

Mr. Twickenham had married above his station in life, and had often boisterously emphasized that fact. Though he had been unfortunate in love, his wife failing to survive their daughter's birth, Mr. Twickenham had been more fortunate in business. Now, only five and forty and in possession of a huge fortune, he had decided it was time to provide a match for himself instead of his daughter. His eye had lit upon his daughter's companion, the widow of a captain under Wellington, Anne Hansen. Her unwillingness had brought about Georgie and Tabby's plan.

"Just leave everything to me. That is, everything but looking dewey-eyed at my beloved brother." Georgina chewed on her bottom lip. "I wish he would write and tell me when he is arriving." Georgina's brother, ten years her senior, had lived in London since he had returned from the war. While she adored him, she was irritated that he treated her and her father so casually, leaving their father lonely.

If Georgina could interest her father in marrying Anne, then the woman would have a protector and a home, and her father would no longer be lonely.

―――――

The cold northerly wind sent a chill up Georgina's back. Though Greenbriar Manor was a snug house, the howling of the wind seemed to seep through its walls. She leaned toward the roaring fire.

"Winter seems to be setting in early, Papa." Her father didn't look up from his book.

"Hmmm?" he finally said, acknowledging his daughter's words. "What did you say, Georgie?"

With a smile, Georgina repeated her statement. When her father was involved in his studies, she did not expect his attention.

"I suppose you are right. Christmas will soon be upon us."

"Not for another six weeks. Do you suppose Nathaniel will come home this winter?" Georgina kept her voice casual, hoping to disguise the importance of her question.

A wry smile on his face, Mr. Denbigh replied, "I do not know, Georgie, my girl. The boy seems to go his own road."

"Oh, Papa." Georgina sighed as she moved from her chair to sit on the floor beside her father and lean her head against his knee.

"Never mind, my dear. While we may miss him, your brother comes from fine stock. He will return home when he is ready to settle down." His fingers stroked her auburn hair, so like his own in his youth.

"It is that stupid Napoleon's fault! If he had not been so hungry for power, Nathaniel would never have gone to war. And England would never have lost so many of its men."

"Aye, the man has much to be responsible for."

Mr. Denbigh returned to his reading, and Georgina stared into the fire, her thoughts focused on her plan. She *needed* Nathaniel to come home. "I hope he returns soon," she muttered to herself.

Despite his preoccupation, Mr. Denbigh noted his daughter's comment with a frown. Georgie usually didn't dwell on problems. He stroked her hair again. "Perhaps he will, my dear. And then you will have someone to tease again."

Georgina smiled in memory. "I did torment him when I was a child, didn't I?"

"*Was* a child?"

"Oh, Papa, you know I am grown up now! You are just as much a tease as anyone!"

A knock at the library door interrupted them. "Enter," Mr. Denbigh called. Wilkins, their butler, opened the door. Before he could announce the guests, however, two men pushed into the room, surrounded with a rush of cold air.

"Nathaniel!" Mr. Denbigh exclaimed, jumping to his feet to hug his son. A younger version of his father's tall, lean frame, Nathaniel warmly returned the embrace.

Georgina was next to greet her brother, her eyes glistening with happiness.

Only after all the exclaiming had died down did Nathaniel Denbigh remember his guest. "Papa, Georgie, I hope you will not mind, but I invited Jason to take Christmas with us."

Georgie turned wide-eyed to stare at the hauntingly familiar grey eyes of the tall, blond man. "Of course not," she replied woodenly.

"We are delighted," Mr. Denbigh added.

Lord Chesterton quickly made his apologies. "I'm sorry if my visit finds you unprepared."

"It is of no importance. Georgie is always prepared," Mr. Denbigh assured his guest.

Lord Chesterton turned to study the person who must be the grown-up version of little Georgie, the child who had followed him everywhere the summer she was eight. He saw a trim young lady with the family auburn hair, brown eyes and glowing cheeks, an accreditable beauty. With a bow, he murmured, "Miss Denbigh, it is a delight to renew our acquaintance."

Georgina swept him her most graceful curtsy. "Thank you, my lord. We are honored to have you as our guest."

"Such formality! Come on, Georgie. 'Tis only Jason. You must not treat him as a stranger." Nathaniel frowned worriedly. He'd hoped his friend would be counted as a member of the family, as he had the summer he had stayed ten years earlier.

Georgina, however, felt ill at ease with Lord Chesterton. In addition to being titled and wealthy, he was, in Georgina's opinion, the most handsome man alive. When he had spent the summer with Nathaniel the year she was eight, she had adored him. Now, faced with a slightly older version and her own adult awareness, she was

tongue-tied. "Of course, J-Jason. Welcome to Greenbriar
Manor."

With another curtsy, Georgina then excused herself to
arrange a room for their guest and to order a substantial
tea in case the two men had not eaten.

As the door closed behind his sister, Nathaniel asked
his father, "Is anything the matter with Georgie?"

"Nothing at all. Won't you be seated?" Mr. Denbigh
said, gesturing to a cherry red chintz-covered armchair
drawn up near the fire. "The wind must have thoroughly
chilled the two of you."

"Oh, we traveled in Jason's new coach. It is well sprung
and quite snug, Papa."

"All the same," Jason said, grinning, "I will take advantage of your hearth. With the departure of the sun, all
warmth seemed to flee my presence."

Once the three men were settled, Mr. Denbigh said, "I
am delighted you have come for Christmas, but I must
confess to be surprised. Have the charms of the city begun
to pall?"

Jason looked ruefully at his friend. "Did you give your
father no warning at all, Nathaniel?"

"This is my home," Nathaniel said indignantly.
"Though perhaps I should have sent you notice. But Georgie practically demanded my appearance for Christmas,
so I assumed you would be expecting us."

"I did not know Georgie had written you, Nathaniel. I
hope you did not feel compelled to abandon your comfortable life in London because of her complaints."

Nathaniel felt a twinge of guilt. "Of course not, Papa.
I have been intending to pay a long visit these many
months. It is just that something always came up."

"This is your home," Mr. Denbigh said as he settled
back in his chair. "You are always welcome, whenever

you arrive. And Jason, if I may call you that, it is a pleasure to have you among us again.''

"Thank you, Mr. Denbigh, and I would prefer that all formality be dismissed between us.''

"Agreed. Ever since my Elizabeth scolded you for your muddy boots, it has seemed ridiculous to use your title,'' Mr. Denbigh said with a smile.

"Please accept my condolences for Mrs. Denbigh's death, sir,'' Jason said. "After both your kindnesses to me, I should have written.''

"Do not give it another thought, my boy,'' Mr. Denbigh said, hoping to ease his guest's discomfort. "After your experiences on the Continent, I am sure you had much on your mind.''

Mr. Denbigh asked about the happenings in London, and the three men chatted, comfortably ensconced in the warmth of the room. They were interrupted by the reappearance of Georgina followed by Wilkins and a retinue of footmen bearing trays.

The two travelers, not having stopped for a final meal in their desire to reach their destination, fell to at once, while Mr. Denbigh and his daughter only took cups of tea. Wiping his mouth, Nathaniel said, "Georgie, you keep house just like Mama.''

With a warm smile, Georgina said, "I can think of no better compliment, Nathaniel. Thank you.''

"I must join Nathaniel in his praise. Food has never tasted better,'' Jason added.

Georgina thought that during her absence from the parlor she had regained her equanimity, but Lord Chesterton's comment had her blushing. "Thank you, Jason. I am glad it pleases you.''

As the new arrivals enjoyed the repast, Georgina could not resist occasional peeps at the man of whom she had such fond memories. When he caught one of her glances, she rushed into speech to cover her embarrassment. "How long will you be able to remain with us, Nathaniel?"

"Oh, Jason and I intend to stay until well after Christmas, Georgie."

Jason's gaze had not left his hostess since he had discovered her looking at him. Now he made a bid for her attention. "You have certainly changed since the last time I saw you, Georgie."

A smile crept onto her solemn face. "I should hope so. I believe I was a rather grubby child who persisted in following your every footstep."

Jason matched her warmth. In that smile, he had discovered the little Georgie he had been so fond of. "I have no complaints, my dear. I have fond memories of that summer."

"Then you must have forgotten the time she pushed you into the stream just as you snagged that huge trout," Nathaniel reminded his friend with a grin.

All three men laughed, but Georgie was embarrassed by her brother's tale. She rose, causing the gentlemen to stand. "I will excuse myself for the evening. It is late and I'm sure the travelers will wish to seek their beds early. Wilkins will show you your room when you are ready to retire, Jason." With a brief curtsy, she left them.

There was an awkward silence before Jason, Lord Chesterton, said, "I somehow have the feeling that Georgie is not pleased with me."

"Don't be ridiculous," Nathaniel said as he poured himself a brandy.

Mr. Denbigh smiled. "Don't concern yourself. What is

amusing to us probably embarrassed Georgie. Young ladies like to maintain their dignity.''

"I will offer my apologies in the morning," Jason said. "I would do nothing to upset her. Memories of home, such as the summer I spent here with Nathaniel and Georgie, made the trials of war more bearable.''

"I'm glad you had something to sustain you. That must have been a difficult time.'' Mr. Denbigh added a silent prayer that both young men had survived. "I am sorry it has been so long since we have seen you. I had hoped to visit with you on our last trip to London.''

"You visited London recently? I know I was away from the city on your visit last spring, but I did not know you had been there since then.'' Jason cast an inquiring look at his friend.

"You were . . . occupied with other things and their visit was short," Nathaniel explained.

Mr. Denbigh laughed. "From Nathaniel's tones, I assume the other thing was a lady. Are you ready to settle down at last, Jason?''

"No, Mr. Denbigh," Jason said, leveling a quelling look at Nathaniel. "I am not ready to be leg-shackled yet. The marriages of my friends do not recommend it.''

"The young ladies expect a gentleman to bow to their every whim, Papa," Nathaniel said. "Even worse, they lay in wait for any unsuspecting male, hoping to trap him into marriage.''

"I am sure you are both quite skilled at evading their stratagems," Mr. Denbigh said with a grin. "But I must admit to looking forward to grandchildren playing about my feet.''

"Since I have no parents to please, there is only the succession to consider. And I believe a distant cousin

in Yorkshire would be overjoyed to know he is next in
line.''

Mr. Denbigh noted his guest's world-weary tones.
''Well, here you will be free from the demands of sophisticated young ladies. There is only Georgie, and her
thoughts turn more toward her mare or that dratted dog
you gave her, Jason. You may relax, knowing you have
left the matrimonial traps behind you in London.''

# Chapter Two

When she came down the stairs for breakfast the next morning, Georgina handed a folded note to the footman dusting the refectory table in the entry hall. "Please deliver this to Miss Twickenham as soon as possible, Albert. It is very important."

"Yes, mum." The young man tucked it in his pocket beneath the apron he wore. "Shall I go right now?"

"Yes, right away, Albert. I will explain to Wilkins."

Delighted with the prospect of a ride, even on such a cold day, Albert grinned his agreement and hurried from the hall, untying his apron as he went.

With a winning smile, Georgina entered the breakfast parlor. "Wilkins, do not be angry with me, but I have enlisted Albert on an important errand. May he finish the hall later?"

Though he rolled his eyes, Wilkins agreed. "It's all right, Miss Georgina. I'll get one of the upstairs maids to do the dusting."

"Thank you, Wilkins," his mistress replied before filling her plate at the sideboard. Her brother was the only one at table, and she greeted him cheerfully as she sat down.

"What important errand is Albert doing for you?" Nathaniel asked as Wilkins left the room.

Georgina knew her plan would work best if her brother remained ignorant of his role. "Oh, it is not really that urgent. I needed a note delivered, and Albert does enjoy being out-of-doors."

"And I thought you had grown up."

"I've certainly had time to do so since your last visit," Georgina said dryly.

Nathaniel said sternly, "I am ten years your senior, young lady. It is not your place to take me to task."

"But, brother, dear, we both know Papa is much too generous to do so." While she was quite serious in her criticism, Georgina loved her brother too much to hold back a smile.

"I know, I know," he agreed with a sigh. "I should have returned earlier, but . . . but I felt so restless, Georgie. And Jason and I lost so many of our friends. I did not want to lose him also."

"Do not be ridiculous. How could you lose Lord Chesterton in London?"

"I am worried about him, Georgie. And you must stop using his title," Nathaniel admonished.

"I forgot. Besides, I am no longer a child. I do not feel I know him well enough to dispense with his title," she said loftily.

"Georgie!" Nathaniel warned, reminding his sister of the days when she had tormented him to play with her.

"If you promise to stay the winter with us, I will do as you request."

"That is blackmail! And besides, I have already said we will stay until after Christmas."

His young sister ignored his response, calmly eating her breakfast. He stared at her in surprise. When he had left for the Continent seven years ago, Georgie was eleven. She would have done anything he requested then. "All right, Georgie, I promise to stay. But I cannot promise for Jason.''

''That's all I ask, Nathaniel,'' she assured him. ''Truly, Papa needs you here to run the estate at least part of the time. He longs to work on his studies. He is writing a book on plant life. As it is, he stays up late writing and gets up early to oversee the work on the estate. I am concerned about him.''

With a sigh, Nathaniel agreed with his sister. ''You are right, Georgie. I have been remiss remaining absent for so long. I will make it up to Papa, I promise.''

Georgina studied his dismal expression. ''Will it be so onerous to remain here in the countryside?''

Nathaniel dismissed her question with a wave of his hand. ''It is not that, Georgie. But—I do not know. I do not even know what I am seeking.''

''If you have not found it in three years of searching in the city, perhaps it has been here all along,'' she said, extending her hand across the table to her brother.

''Perhaps, little sister. I pray you are right.'' He squeezed her hand. ''I must tell you about Jason. I invited him to accompany me because—''

''Good morning,'' the subject of their conversation said as he entered the room. Noticing their clasped hands and serious expressions he asked, ''Do you wish to remain in private? I could—''

''No, of course not, Jason,'' Nathaniel assured him, jumping up to guide him to the sideboard. ''Please help yourself. We are delighted to have you join us.''

Though Jason acquiesced to his friend, his eyes remained fixed on the young lady, seeking her permission. Georgina saw her brother's anxious look, and, despite her frustration at being interrupted at such a pregnant moment, she smiled. "You must count us as family, Jason, and not stand on ceremony."

She was rewarded by smiles from both gentlemen.

"Thank you, Georgina. I was afraid last evening I had somehow offended you. You left our company much too early, unlike the summer I spent here so long ago."

Georgina's cheeks flushed. "I am no longer a child, Jason, and I find it embarrassing to be reminded of my behavior. You must have thought me impossible."

"I thought you a darling, Georgie, and I carried wonderful memories of your sweet face with me." Jason stared into the older version of that face, entranced by her smile.

Nathaniel brought them back to reality. "And in return, you left that dratted dog. Do you still have it, Georgie?"

"Of course I do. Chester is in my bedchamber at this very moment. Papa has forbidden him the breakfast parlor because he insists on begging for food."

"You named him Chester?" Jason asked in amusement.

"I thought it appropriate at the time. I didn't think Jason a good name for a dog." Georgina's warm smile lit up her brown eyes and Jason thought she looked beautiful.

"I notice you are dressed for riding. Have you already gone, or do you intend to ride after breakfast?" he asked.

"I usually ride after breakfast. Would either of you care to join me?" Georgie asked.

Both men expressed an interest. "It would be a good idea to see some of the estate if I am to take over the running of it," Nathaniel added.

Jason looked up from his plate, a frown on his face. "What do you mean, Nathaniel?"

''Georgie has been telling me how much I am needed here. I have decided to stay at least for the winter.'' Since his friend continued to frown, Nathaniel added, ''I hope you will remain here with us, Jason. After all, there is nothing to draw you back to town.''

Much to Georgina's disappointment, their guest did not respond favorably. ''I do not believe I shall be able to absent myself from society for that long.''

''Oh, come now, Jason—''

''I am sure country life will seem quite boring compared to the sophistication of London,'' Georgina agreed quietly. Before either man could respond, she murmured an excuse and sprang from the table to leave the room, afraid she would not be able to hide her dismay if she stayed. She should have known better than to think Jason would be content with the peaceful life at Greenbriar Manor after London.

''I do not mean to offend Georgina,'' Jason said regretfully.

Nathaniel stared at his friend in exasperation. ''I thought you were bored with town life? Why did you respond in such a way?''

''I just did not want to impose on your father's hospitality for such a long time, Nathaniel. After all, I arrived uninvited.''

''Surely you cannot doubt your welcome?'' Nathaniel demanded.

''No, of course not. But I thought you would return to town with me. We have been together for so long.''

Nathaniel nodded. ''I know. That is why I do not want you to leave. But I can no longer avoid my responsibilities. I am needed here.'' He paused before adding, ''Stay as long as you can, Jason.''

"Of course," Jason agreed. "And I will make my peace with Georgina on our ride. Shall we go?"

Both men rose to follow in Georgina's footsteps.

———

Georgie enjoyed her morning ride a great deal more than usual. Most of the time she led a lonely life, only enlivened by Tabitha's visits or the infrequent social occasions in the county.

After their return, she changed into a pale green sprig muslin that lit up her auburn curls and hurried to the housekeeper's room. She was already behind schedule because her brother had wanted to see as much of the estate as possible in one morning.

When she emerged from planning the menus to suit their additional numbers and ensuring serenity reigned below stairs with the two new valets, Wilkins was opening the door to Tabitha Twickenham and her companion, Anne Hansen.

"Tabby, Anne, I'm so glad you have come. Thank you, Wilkins. I'll escort our guests to the parlor. Perhaps we might have some tea?"

Taking both ladies by the arm, Georgina seated them in cozy chairs before the fire. "Won't you agree to stay for luncheon?" she asked, still standing.

"Oh, no, Georgina, we do not want to intrude," Anne said in her quiet voice. "Tabby insisted you wanted to see some of my drawings. She said you might need them in the reader you are preparing for the children."

"That's true. But you must dine with us. After all, it is a cold ride and you have been so kind to come at once. I'll return in just a moment." With a smile, Georgina walked gracefully from the room. As soon as the door was closed, she hiked her skirts and ran down the long center hallway to her father's library.

Before she could reach her destination, however, Jason emerged from the morning room. His surprised look halted her in her tracks. Dropping her skirts, she dipped a small curtsy and would have gone on her way were it not for his hand on her arm.

"Is there some emergency, Georgina?"

"No, Jason. I am just in a hurry. If you'll excuse me—"

Jason stood in the hallway grinning even as Georgina entered the library. Little Georgie. She had been so much on her dignity since his arrival that he had caught only glimpses of the child he had known. Her behavior just now told him the child was lurking just below that polished surface.

In London, the young ladies never shed their awe of his rank and fortune. He could swear night was day and day night and nary a one would contradict him. And never, never would they willingly leave his side for another man, much less their fathers. But he knew just how shallow their intentions were.

"And you will join us in just a moment, won't you, Papa? You will not forget?" she called back over her shoulder before pulling the door to behind her. She reached for her skirts, ready to race to her next destination, when she found Jason had not yet departed. "Oh, good, you are still here. Would you and Nathaniel join us in the parlor? I would like you both to meet my particular friend who has come to call."

"Of course. We would be delighted," he replied, curious about the excitement he saw in her face. Had she been a London miss, he would have been suspicious, but, after all, this was little Georgie.

"Good." With that absentminded response, Georgina hurried back to the parlor.

"I apologize for being away so long, but I thought to ask Papa to join us. He has quite an interest in plants also, you know," Georgina explained to the others. "You *have* met my father, haven't you, Anne?" She gave the girl a pointed look.

"Yes, Georgina, of course I have." Anne clutched her drawings in her lap. "But I am sure your father will not be interested in my sketches. I wish you had not disturbed him."

Georgina was surprised to note signs of nervousness in the normally calm Anne. She looked at her friend, Tabby, who, having fulfilled her role so far with great distinction, was toasting her slippers before the fire.

Not only had Tabby managed to convince Anne she should come to Greenbriar Manor, but she had also persuaded her to wear her new lavender walking dress that complimented Anne's trim figure and winter-reddened cheeks.

Tabby, herself, knowing her role as lovesick admirer, had chosen a sky blue gown trimmed in fine lace. Anne had thought it excessively fine for a morning call, but as Tabby pointed out, their social life was quite limited. She must wear her new gowns when she could.

"Papa will be delighted with them, Anne," Georgie said confidently. "The details of your paintings are so life-like. Do not be the least bit concerned," Georgina assured the older woman. The door opened at that moment, but Georgina was disappointed to discover only her brother and his friend. She was eager for her father to arrive.

"Oh, I had not told you that my brother returned last evening," Georgina exclaimed. She rose and extended her hand to her brother. "Anne, Tabby, may I present my brother, Mr. Nathaniel Denbigh, and his friend, Lord Chesterton."

"May we join you, ladies?" Nathaniel asked, seating himself beside the older woman when they agreed. He was not sure why his sister had demanded his presence, but he was happy to attend her tea party. "Do you live nearby?"

Anne, her nervousness over her drawings forgotten, responded smoothly. "Mr. Twickenham, Tabitha's father, purchased the estate to the east of yours last January, sir."

"Mr. Buxton's estate?" Nathaniel demanded, a frown on his face.

"I am not sure . . ." Anne began, her eyes signaling to Georgina for assistance.

"Yes?" Georgina responded, her mind still on her father's absence.

"Was Mr. Twickenham's estate previously owned by a Mr. Buxton?" Anne asked. "Your brother has asked, but I did not come to the neighborhood until March."

"Yes, of course it was Mr. Buxton's estate. Do you not remember, Nathaniel? I wrote you that he passed away. After all, he was almost in his eightieth year."

"No, I do not remember," Nathaniel said with a frown.

"I wrote you about it, Nathaniel," Georgina repeated.

"Georgie, Papa knew I wanted to purchase Mr. Buxton's estate should it become available," Nathaniel said, a little puzzled.

Her brother's wishes were of no consequence to Georgina at the moment. "I am sorry, Nathaniel. Perhaps you should discuss it with Papa *later*." The heavy emphasis on the last word reminded Nathaniel of their guests.

"My apologies, ladies," he said. "I was taken by surprise."

The subject was forgotten as Wilkins opened the door and led in three footmen, each bearing a large tray. Georgina, eager for her tea party to be a success, rose to direct the proceedings. Unfortunately an uninvited guest raced in. Georgie turned her head just in time to see a streak of gold enter the room before it entwined itself with the various feet of the footmen, toppling them in order. The resulting crash, coupled with flying dishes and bits of scones and tea cakes, ended the tea party.

Mr. Denbigh arrived at the open door to be greeted by an astounding scene accompanied by the sound of an unapologetic Chester's bark. "My, my, there seems to have been a mishap. I trust no one is seriously injured?"

For a moment the guests had been frozen in horror. Now wakened from their trance, everyone began talking at once. The footmen picked themselves up, having sustained only bruises, and began gathering the ruins of tea under a stern Wilkins's eye. The ladies inspected the damage to their costumes occasioned by flying debris, pushing aside crumbs, and hoping there were no stains.

"I apologize for arriving so tardily, Georgie, though my valet will be most grateful." He covered his mouth so the others would not be offended by his huge smile.

Nathaniel stood, a blob of clotted cream hanging to his curls. "I do not even know what happened. One moment we were talking, and the next we were covered with our tea. Are you ladies all right?"

All three women struggled to hold back a chuckle at his appearance. The knowledge that they were in no better condition sobered them somewhat.

"I daresay this yapping mutt had something to do with it," Mr. Denbigh said. "Wilkins, would you summon a footman to take this creature to the stables?"

Wilkins, having sorted out his helpers, said with outrage, "It was that dog's fault, Mr. Denbigh! He upset everything."

Georgina, already cuddling the golden setter against her, patted his head reassuringly. "Truly, Wilkins, he did not mean to cause any difficulties. Molly was supposed to keep him in my chamber.''

"Never mind, Wilkins. You are not to blame,'' Mr. Denbigh assured the butler. With a sniff, the man turned back to his duties.

"Georgina, if you will take your guests to your room to repair what damage may have occurred, I'll have Wilkins bring up another tea tray to you there. I hope you ladies will stay to luncheon?''

Mr. Denbigh's charming smile made both ladies forget the stains their new gowns had suffered. Accepting their second invitation to luncheon, they both stood to follow Georgina from the room, and Anne's forgotten drawings spilled to the floor.

Mr. Denbigh, the only person capable of quick movement in the aftermath of the debacle, knelt to rescue the papers. Catching sight of the drawings, he paused to examine several of them closely.

"These are exquisite, Mrs. Hansen. Did you draw these plants?''

"Why, yes, Mr. Denbigh. Georgie asked me to bring some over. She thought she might use them in her book for the children,'' Anne explained dismissively.

"I did not know you were so talented. I would love to see any others you might have, if you would not mind.'' Mr. Denbigh eyed the woman in appreciation.

"I would be delighted to show you if—if you are sure they would not bore you,'' Anne stammered, her cheeks growing warm again.

"On the contrary. I would be enchanted to see them. Now, Georgina will take you upstairs to recover from this regrettable incident. We will visit at luncheon.''

Georgina wasted no time in leading the ladies from the room, eager to escape her tea party. Even though it had appeared to be a disaster, she had accomplished her goal.

Nathaniel and Jason remained standing amidst the debris. Mr. Denbigh grinned at the two of them. "You certainly don't resemble a pair of town beaux now, gentlemen," he teased.

"Papa," Nathaniel protested ruefully, "*we* are Corinthians, never town beaux."

"Ah, of course, I stand corrected. But I believe you'd best repair the damage before luncheon, or our fair guests will lose their appetites."

Both young men grinned and turned to leave, picking their way between the footmen now retrieving the farflung tea. At the door, Nathaniel paused. "Papa, Miss Twickenham's father bought Mr. Buxton's estate?"

"Yes, immediately after his death."

Nathaniel paused before saying lightly, "I had always hoped we could add his acres to ours when that time came."

Mr. Denbigh eyed his son. "I did consider it, Nathaniel, but I could not manage both estates. Before I had time to contact you, Mr. Twickenham purchased it."

Realizing he had only himself to blame, Nathaniel nodded and would have gone on his way, but his father stopped him.

"Of course, there may still be a way to acquire the Buxton estate."

Nathaniel turned eagerly toward his father.

"You have only to marry Miss Twickenham. She is her father's only child," he said with a straight face.

As Nathaniel stared at his parent as if he had lost his mind, Jason stepped in to say, "But we left London to avoid just such things, remember, Mr. Denbigh?"

"Yes, of course, of course. It was just a thought," Mr.

Denbigh said with a smile. He stepped over an upended scone on the Aubusson carpet and clasped his son by the shoulders. "Never mind, my boy. We have land enough without the Buxton estate. You two go up and wipe the cream from your faces. I will see you at luncheon."

# Chapter Three

Despite her father's genial nature during luncheon, Georgina dreaded her interview with him afterwards. She was sure he would condemn Chester permanently to the stables. He had threatened to do so several times.

Mr. Denbigh called for her to enter the study after her knock, and Georgina slipped into the room, her head down.

"Surely I am not such an ogre as to browbeat you, am I, Georgie?" her father's amused voice inquired.

"Oh, Papa." Georgie ran to the sofa where her father awaited her. He held out his arms and she gladly submitted herself to his hug. "I truly did tell Molly to keep Chester in my chamber. It was an accident that he escaped."

"I'm sure it was, my dear. But society will shun us if we drown them in tea."

"It won't happen again, Papa, I promise."

"Very well," Mr. Denbigh conceded with a sigh, much to Georgina's relief.

"Thank you, Papa," she exclaimed, giving him a kiss and jumping to her feet.

Before she could leave, her father added, "Nathaniel was disappointed that I did not buy the Buxton estate."

"I know."

With a cautious look at his daughter, Mr. Denbigh added, "I suggested he marry Miss Twickenham if he still wanted it."

Georgina's eyes widened. *What a marvelous idea!* "What did Nathaniel say in response, Papa?"

"Your brother does not appear to be ready to settle down," Mr. Denbigh explained with a twinkle in his eye. "Though he voiced no objection to Miss Twickenham personally."

"And why should he? Tabby is quite beautiful and—and very sweet."

"I agree, my dear, but I must warn you that your brother and Jason have mentioned to me that they have retreated to the country because they are tired of the marital traps constantly being sprung on them in London."

Georgina avoided her father's eyes. Thank goodness she had not confessed her plans for her father to Nathaniel! She stole a look at him, but his gaze had returned to his books. "The behavior of the ladies of the *ton* has nothing to do with me, Papa."

"And I assured the two gentlemen they had nothing with which to be concerned."

Her father's smile removed some of Georgina's worry. "Of course, Papa."

Mr. Denbigh rose from the couch. "Good. I was impressed with Mrs. Hansen's talent, by the way. Her drawings of plant life are exquisite."

"Yes, they are, are they not?" Georgina agreed eagerly. "And she is a most pleasant woman."

"If only she were a little younger, she would make a perfect wife for Nathaniel," Mr. Denbigh murmured, an abstract look in his eyes.

"But, Papa, she is forty years old! That is much too old for Nathaniel."

"Is she that old? I had not realized—she looks younger."

Since her father was already studying one of the books on his desk, Georgina was sure he was no longer thinking about Anne Hansen. With an exasperated sigh, she walked over and kissed him on his cheek before turning to the door. He surprised her as she opened it, however.

"Thank you, Georgie."

"For what, Papa?"

"For being such a good daughter. Now, be off with you."

Georgina closed the door with a smile on her face. She had the most understanding father imaginable—even if he was easily distracted by his studies.

———

When only her father and she were dining, Georgina frequently ordered the meal served in the breakfast parlor, preferring its intimacy over the stately elegance of the dining room. However, with the added company of her brother and Jason, the evening meal took place in the dining room with polished silver and crystal adding sparkle to the candlelight.

Georgina herself was more elegantly dressed than normal, though she supposed her toilette was nothing compared to what the men were used to in London. Still, the deep rose silk gown she wore was one of her favorites from her last shopping trip to London. Its simple lines flattered her slender figure, and the low neckline with its white lace trim framed her perfect complexion.

"I say, Georgie, you look superb in that gown," Nathaniel exclaimed as she entered the parlor. "I wouldn't have thought you could wear that color with your hair."

"Thank you, brother dear. It is an unusual combination, isn't it? You gentlemen look very elegant this evening also.'' She paused but couldn't resist adding with a giggle, ''You appear more sophisticated without cream adorning your hair.''

The three men laughed at the reminder of the morning.

Once they were seated at the table and Wilkins began serving bowls of consommé, Georgina asked her brother conversationally, ''Did you like Miss Twickenham and her companion Mrs. Hansen?''

''They seemed pleasant enough,'' he replied as he lifted his spoon to his mouth.

Jason leaned forward. ''They are both quite attractive, don't you think, Mr. Denbigh?''

For the first time since his arrival, he was surprised to see his hostess positively beaming at him. He frowned in puzzlement, wondering what he had done to earn such approbation.

Mr. Denbigh didn't look up from his soup. ''Yes, and Mrs. Hansen is quite talented, also.''

''You are referring to her drawings?'' Nathaniel asked.

''Yes, they are wonderful.'' He took a sip of soup. ''Georgie, I would love to have Mrs. Hansen make some drawings to accompany my scribblings. Would she be offended if I offered to pay her?''

Georgina had hoped the drawings would catch her father's attention, but she wanted a different response. ''I don't know, Papa. Anne is a generous person. She will probably offer to do them for free even though she needs the money.''

''She has no husband to support her?'' Jason asked.

''Her husband was a captain in the cavalry,'' Georgie said. ''He was killed in Spain fighting the French about five years ago. Since then, Anne has worked as a companion or governess.''

Mr. Denbigh frowned. "I thought perhaps she was a distant relative of Tabitha's. That settles it. I cannot allow her to make the drawings unless she lets me pay her for her work."

Georgina hoped Anne would not be offended by her father's determination to pay her. If she didn't do the drawings for him, then it was unlikely the two would ever notice each other. "I could explain your offer to Anne, Papa. I think she would enjoy doing the work."

"That might be best, Georgie. But you make sure she understands that I must pay her for her efforts."

"Yes, Papa. I'll ride over tomorrow after breakfast and talk with her," Georgina assured him eagerly, not wanting to waste any time.

"I will accompany you, if you don't mind, Georgina," Jason said. His grey eyes remained trained on her face as he added, "I enjoyed our ride this morning very much." Though he had vowed disdain of women's adulation and pursuit, Lord Chesterton expected some kind of reaction from his hostess.

Georgina, however, was more interested in her brother's company because of the seed her father had planted, and she turned eagerly to him, a question in her eyes.

"And I will go, also," he responded to her satisfaction. "I would like to see if this Mr. Twickenham has made any changes on the estate."

Georgina rang for the next course, but her thoughts were on more important matters. She peeked at her brother and wished she had thought to ask Tabby her opinion of him. In the past women had always found him romantic in appearance, though, in her opinion, Jason, with his golden locks and steely grey eyes, was the more attractive. She was sure his tall muscular figure had as much to do with his reputation among the ladies as did his title and fortune.

But for the sake of her plan, she hoped Tabby did not feel the same as her.

"Did you not find Miss Twickenham attractive?" Georgina prompted her brother.

"She is most attractive," Jason responded instead of Nathaniel. "Though I find her too much the ingenue."

Georgina frowned, darting a look at her brother, who showed greater interest in his baked chicken than the young lady under discussion. "Some gentlemen prefer the innocence and charm of a young lady to a—a more experienced sophisticate," she replied stiffly.

"I did not mean to offend, Georgina," Jason said. "I simply meant she seems a shy young woman."

"So would you be if you had been treated as she was."

"What do you mean?" Nathaniel asked, his attention caught by her words.

"Her father is a cit who made a huge fortune. When Tabby was barely sixteen, he took her to London for the season without any preparation at all. The woman he hired to chaperone her lived on the outskirts of society and scarcely knew a fashionable dress from a turnip. The two of them shoved Tabby out among the bucks of London society and she was treated horribly."

"That is most unfortunate," Nathaniel commented.

At least, Georgina thought, she had drawn her brother's attention away from his dinner.

"Anyway, Tabby was poorly treated and now believes she is not attractive or worthy of a proper marriage. Her father is a cit, it's true, but her mother's family is perfectly respectable. But no matter how often I tell her, I have yet to convince her," Georgina finished, her frustration with her friend obvious.

"Perhaps she should return to London," Nathaniel said

wryly. "Ladies with fortunes are scarce since the war ended. I suspect she would have a better reception now."

"I don't think Tabitha would care for that," Georgina said carefully.

Her father cleared his throat and she introduced a new topic for discussion.

Georgie hoped she hadn't been too obvious. She must not draw attention to her plans.

―――――――

The next morning Georgina sought out Albert again with another note to be delivered. She wanted to warn her friend of the impending visit from her, her brother, and Jason. It was important that Tabitha look her best—though, of course, Georgina could not explain that to Tabitha. One hint of a *real* match between Tabitha and Nathaniel, and Tabby would take to her bed and never show her face again.

She entered the breakfast room and discovered both her escorts already dining, along with her father. Donning a pleasant smile, she seated herself at the foot of the small table and played her role of hostess to perfection, intent on creating a harmonious mood for the morning.

"Are you sure you will not accompany us, Papa?" Georgina asked as they rose from the table.

"Thank you, child, but I must examine the north meadow with Judson. He wants to plow it up and sow wheat." Judson had been their estate manager since before Georgina's birth.

Nathaniel frowned. "Shall I go with him in your place, Papa?"

Georgina held her breath, waiting for her father's reply.

"No, son, accompany your sister. If Mrs. Hansen agrees to do those drawings for me, I will be turning a lot of work over to you."

Though her brother accepted her father's decision, he appeared in deep thought most of the way over to the Buxton estate. Only when they were on the property did he snap out of his self-absorption.

Georgina had been maintaining an effortless conversation with Jason, amazed at how easily their camaraderie of old was reestablished, when her brother interrupted them. "Look at that field. Does Mr. Twickenham have an estate manager?"

Georgina understood her brother's irritation. The estate had sadly deteriorated in the past few months. Mr. Twickenham was a city man who had no interest in running a producing estate. She and her father had noticed the disastrous results of his inattention, and the estate manager Twickenham had hired knew almost as little as his master.

"Yes, Mr. Shindler is the estate manager," she said.

"He's not a local?" Nathaniel asked.

"No, Mr. Twickenham hired him in London," Georgina explained with a grin, knowing her brother would explode.

"What? The idiot hired a city man to run the estate?" Nathaniel howled. "Surely you jest, Georgie. No one could be so stupid!"

"Tabby said the man had references of previous work on estates and came highly recommended."

"Even I, who spends most of his time in the city, can see that this estate is in poor condition. Was it like this during the previous owner's lifetime?" Jason asked.

"No," Nathaniel growled. "Mr. Buxton was a fine farmer."

"The last year he was not as active as before, but even at his age, Mr. Buxton maintained his estate," Georgina assured Jason. "The man Mr. Twickenham hired has only passing knowledge of farming or work. He does little enough of either to warrant a salary.''

"Has Mr. Twickenham been informed?" Nathaniel demanded.

Georgina smiled as she said, "Mr. Twickenham spends most of his time in the city, and I'm afraid he is not one who listens well.''

"Well, he must listen to me. It is a sin to allow such a fine estate to go to ruin,'' Nathaniel said firmly.

Georgina closed her eyes in frustration. It was all very well for her hot-headed brother to be concerned about the land, but she didn't think Mr. Twickenham would welcome criticism. And if he became upset with her brother, it was entirely possible he would forbid Tabby to visit her. And that would ruin everything!

"Perhaps, since Mr. Twickenham is seldom here, you might visit with Mr. Shindler. I'm sure he would appreciate any hints you might give him about the land. After all, you are a native and he is newly arrived.''

"That's a good idea, Georgie. I'll ask Miss Twickenham if I might meet him today,'' Nathaniel said. "It's probably that the farmers hereabout have been reluctant to talk to him. You know how slow they are to accept newcomers,'' Nathaniel said enthusiastically.

Jason frowned. "I never noticed it when I spent that summer here.''

"That is because you were a friend just visiting,'' Nathaniel assured him. "The farmers here pride themselves on their efficient farming methods and their crops. They may be reluctant to share their secrets with Mr. Shindler. But I will be glad to help him.''

Georgina remained silent. Her evaluation of Mr. Shindler indicated the man would not want any help if it meant

he would have to exert himself. And he certainly would
not want anyone around who might realize he was less
than honest in his dealings. While she was not sure that
he was cheating Mr. Twickenham, she did know several
of the local people would no longer deal with the man
because of his shady practices.

But if her brother confined his advice to the estate manager and did not meet Mr. Twickenham, perhaps her plan
would not be affected.

═══════

Georgina's note had thrown the two women at the Twickenham residence into a frenzy. Tabitha, knowing Georgina's plan, contemplated her role in it all with discomfort.
Mr. Nathaniel Denbigh, with his warm brown eyes and
perfect features, had played a large role in her dreams the
night before. For some reason to pretend infatuation when
she was already attracted to the man seemed even more
difficult.

Seeing her companion's gaze on her face, Tabitha willed
the blush in her cheeks to recede, to no avail.

Anne asked, "Are you pleased Georgina is bringing her
brother and their guest to call?"

"It—it is always pleasant to have guests," Tabitha said
stiffly, uncomfortable in her role as actress.

Anne dropped her eyes to the needlework she was ab-
sentmindedly pursuing. "Both gentlemen are most handsome," she observed, flashing a look at the young woman
beside her.

"Yes, they are. Mr. Denbigh is the most handsome
gentleman I have ever seen," Tabby admitted with a sigh,
falling into her role with a vengeance. "Though, of
course, Lord Chesterton is—is most handsome also," she
added.

Then Tabitha grew concerned that her praise of either gentleman might arouse Anne's interest, ruining Georgina's plans. "But neither are as attractive as Mr. Denbigh!"

"You are attracted to Georgie's father?" Anne exclaimed.

"No! No, of course not. He is too old—that is, he is more mature than—I never said that. But if I were older, I would think—some women might say he is attractive."

"Yes, I quite agree," Anne replied, but she was frowning.

"You do?" Tabby asked eagerly.

"Tabby, I am content. Do not worry yourself with my future. Your father is most concerned with your marriage, you know."

"Has he sent you another letter?" Tabby asked, her heart sinking. Only last month her father had written Anne asking her to further any kind of match for his daughter, since she had failed so miserably in London. He no longer wished to be plagued by an unmarried daughter.

"No, my dear, I have heard nothing more from your father," Anne said, "and he is wrong to say such things. You are a beautiful and talented young woman. It is your father's fault that your season was not successful."

Though her soft, pink lips quivered, Tabitha managed a smile. "You and Georgie are both so kind."

"Nonsense. Kindness has nothing to do with it. I have come to love and appreciate you, Tabby, as if you were the child I never had. I cannot bear for him to hurt you."

The two women clasped hands, but the opening of the door by their butler brought them to attention.

"Miss Twickenham, Miss Denbigh and her brother and

Lord Chesterton have come to call. Shall I show them in?''

"Yes, please, Slocum.''

"Perhaps," Anne whispered with a warm smile, "we shall find you a husband in the neighborhood after all.''

Tabitha's startled look was ignored.

# Chapter Four

"Would you care for more tea?" Tabby asked all her guests, though her eyes dwelled only on Mr. Denbigh.

Georgina watched her friend intently. Tabby was the dearest creature, but she had not thought playacting among her talents. However, either Tabitha was an incredible actress, or she was greatly attracted to Nathaniel. Georgina's delighted smile turned to a frown as she noted Jason staring intently at the couple. "I believe Lord Chesterton would like a second cup," she suggested, in an attempt to distract him.

"Oh! Oh, yes, of course," Tabby agreed, swinging around to face the surprised guest, the silver teapot waving wildly in her hand.

Jason extended his cup in self-defense, since he was seated beside the hostess, and accepted another cup of unwanted tea. "Thank you, Miss Twickenham."

As Jason turned back to continue his conversation with Anne, Nathaniel said, "Miss Twickenham, I would like to meet your man of business. I would like to offer some suggestions."

Anne and Tabitha shared a look of concern before Tabitha said, "That is most generous of you, Mr. Denbigh, but—Mr. Shindler is difficult. He does not take advice well."

"Does your father realize how poorly managed your fields are? Surely he would be concerned, as a businessman, to see his investment dwindle," Nathaniel persisted, unable to be subtle.

Again the two ladies exchanged a glance. "Mr. Twickenham would not believe you, sir," Anne said, "though your concern is most appreciated. I, myself, having been raised in the country, have recognized the man's inadequacies, but Mr. Twickenham refuses to admit he might have made a mistake."

Lord Chesterton said, "Though I do not agree, perhaps it is the generally held wisdom that women do not understand such things that causes Mr. Twickenham to respond so."

"That is stupid!" Georgina protested.

"I said I do not believe it, Georgina, but there are those in society who think women only suitable for wiving and providing heirs," Jason added, an amused look on his face.

Nathaniel hastily intervened. "I still would like to meet Mr. Shindler, Miss Twickenham. I promise I will not cause any difficulties."

Georgina recalled the original purpose of their visit. "Why do you not take the two gentlemen to the stables and show them around, Tabby? Perhaps Mr. Shindler will be there. I need to discuss something with Anne, anyway."

Tabitha looked at Anne for guidance and received a nod. She gracefully stood and the men followed.

The two remaining ladies watched the others depart. Before Georgina could speak, after the door closed, Anne asked, "Georgie, does your brother or Lord Chesterton have any romantic interests in London?"

Georgina stared at her blankly. She dropped her eyes to

smooth the cuff on her blue wool riding habit before she asked anxiously, "Anne, *you* are not interested in either of them?"

"Do not be absurd, child. They are both quite young. I was thinking of Tabby. You know how important it is for her to marry soon. That father of hers has no love for his daughter."

"I also have a plan for Tabby's future," Georgina said eagerly. "My brother—that is, Tabby seems attracted to Nathaniel and, though Papa says he is not yet ready to marry—"

"No gentleman ever is," Anne commented wryly.

"Yes, well, I thought I might promote a match between them."

"You would not object to your brother marrying Tabby?"

"Of course not!" Georgina exclaimed. "I would love having her as my sister. But my brother is used to town ways and—and sophisticated women. Do you think he is attracted to her?"

"Not yet. But if we encourage them . . . ?" Anne suggested as she watched Georgina closely.

"But we must be careful," Georgina said. "My father warned me that Nathaniel and Jason have retired to the country because they were tired of the London ladies' attempts to trap them into marriage."

"Yes, of course, we must not do that," Anne said. "But we could encourage them."

"I think we should," Georgina agreed. She chewed her lip as if thinking. "I know! I have a marvelous idea that will throw Nathaniel and Tabitha in each other's company constantly."

She shot a speculative look at Anne. "My father was most impressed with your illustrations. As you know, he is studying plant life and would like for you to draw some sketches to accompany his writing.''

''Oh, how marvelous,'' Anne exclaimed, her blue eyes lighting up. ''I would love to be of assistance to your father.''

''He needs your help,'' Georgina assured her. ''However, he insists he must pay you for your efforts.''

''Don't be ridiculous,'' Anne said, frowning. ''I draw because I enjoy it. And your father is a neighbor. I would never charge him for my drawings.''

''Then he will not accept them.''

''But, Georgina, I cannot take money from your father.''

''I don't see why not. We always pay for services rendered.''

''I am not a cit, that is why!'' Anne snapped, for once losing her remarkable calm.

''I never meant you were, Anne. But Papa understands your situation and—''

''What do you mean? What have you told him?''

''Only that you must support yourself by acting as governess or companion since your husband's death,'' Georgina assured her. ''He was most impressed by your fortitude, Anne, and your drawings would certainly help Papa. And if Papa turned his attention to his book, Nathaniel would take over the estate instead of returning to London.''

''Oh, Georgie, I do not know what to do! It goes against the grain to sell my art, but . . . but it would provide a nest egg in case I was dismissed from my present position.'' Anne chewed on her bottom lip.

''Surely Mr. Twickenham won't fire you.''

With a wry smile, Anne said, ''He may. He does not

like my standing up for his daughter. Nor does he like my refusing his advances.''

''Men!'' Georgina exclaimed with an understanding nod of her head. ''You must work with Papa. I will handle the fee so that it will not be awkward for you, Anne, but it truly will help Papa and me. But even more importantly, that is part of my plan to bring Nathaniel and Tabby together.''

''And if your brother should discover an interest in Tabby, that would solve *my* problem. She would then be removed from her father's authority.''

''But it would leave you without a job,'' Georgina reminded her.

''Yes, but I would have a nest egg to carry me until my next employment,'' Anne said. ''And I would not have to withstand Mr. Twickenham's heavy-handed courtship. With so many benefits,'' Anne added, ''tell your father I will be delighted to work with him.''

''Good. Will you begin tomorrow? If you arrive right after breakfast, you may spend the entire day. And,'' Georgina added with a delightfully scheming smile, ''I will entertain Tabby—along with my brother and Jason. It will even out the numbers.''

Tabitha led her guests down the cobblestone path to the large stables set a short distance from the house. She was quite conscious of Mr. Denbigh on her left, but each time she glanced at him, he was staring ahead, a fierce frown on his brow. When the man on her other side spoke, she jumped in surprise.

''Have you always lived in the country, Miss Twickenham?'' Jason asked.

''Oh! No, my lord. I—I spent my childhood in Portsmouth. That is where my father's first factory is located.

And then I attended school in Bath until I moved to London.''

"Your father resides in London now?" Nathaniel asked in angry tones.

"Yes, sir," Tabitha whispered, distressed by Nathaniel's anger.

"Have you discussed the estate with your father?"

"Nathaniel, Miss Twickenham is not responsible for the condition of the estate," Jason reminded his friend.

"Of course not! I apologize, Miss Twickenham. I did not mean to imply—"

"Please, Mr. Denbigh, it is all right. It is just that my father does not visit often, and if he will not listen to Anne, he will listen to no one." Tabitha bowed her head.

"He seems a most unnatural father," Nathaniel muttered.

"No, he is like most fathers. You must not mind Nathaniel, Miss Twickenham. He is blessed with the kindest of all parents," Jason commented.

Tabitha smiled at his words. "Mr. Denbigh is very kind, isn't he?"

"Well, we are all in agreement about that," Nathaniel said, dismissing such nonsensical topics and returning to one close to his heart. "When is your father next expected to visit?"

"I do not know," Tabitha replied, ducking her head once more.

As the trio approached the stables, a stooped old man greeted his mistress. "Good morning, miss."

"Good morning, Jacob," Tabitha said.

Before she could ask for the estate manager, Mr. Denbigh spoke to the man. "Jacob, do you have no greeting for me? It's Nathaniel Denbigh."

"Mr. Nathaniel?" the man exclaimed, leaning closer. "That be you?"

Nathaniel reached out to clasp the man by the shoulders. "Yes, Jacob, it's me. How are you?"

The other two waited as Nathaniel conversed with the old man of memories past.

Finally, Tabitha asked, "Jacob, Mr. Denbigh wished to meet Mr. Shindler. Is he here in the stables?"

"Yes'm, he be 'ere, wi' his feet propped up as usual," the stableman growled.

Tabitha wisely ignored his words. "Would you ask him to join us, please, Jacob?"

Nathaniel gave his hostess an approving glance. She treated her servants kindly. Though he had been raised to do so himself, his foray into the world had taught him that such behavior was a rarity.

It was not long before they were joined by Mr. Shindler. Nathaniel watched him approach, his shirt dirty and unlaced, his breeches stained and straining at the seams, and his face unshaven. Because Nathaniel considered her shy, he was surprised to see Tabitha take charge of the introductions.

"Mr. Shindler, our guests wished to ask some questions about the estate, and I thought you might assist them. Gentlemen, may I present Mr. Shindler, the estate manager. Mr. Shindler, this is Lord Chesterton and our neighbor, Mr. Denbigh."

Despite her gracious introduction, the slovenly man only grunted. Nathaniel gazed at him steely-eyed until he shuffled his feet and half tucked in his shirt-tail. "Yes'm, 'course, I'll be glad to answer questions."

Alcoholic fumes drifted from the man's breath. Tabitha's cheeks flushed. "Mr. Shindler, you have been drinking. You will excuse yourself and report to the house in half an hour appropriately dressed and sober.''

All three men were struck by the sternness in the young lady's words. Tabitha turned to go before the estate manager recovered. But he reached out a dirty hand to grasp her arm. ''Here now. You've no call to talk to me like that! I work for your pa, not for some uppity society miss.''

Before Tabitha or Jason could respond, Nathaniel Denbigh planted a facer on Mr. Shindler's disreputable mug and the man crumpled at Tabitha's feet.

''Oh, no!'' Tabitha gasped. ''Papa will be furious.''

''Surely, Miss Twickenham, your father would not allow this man to paw his only daughter,'' Nathaniel demanded, outraged. ''No gentleman would stand for such.''

Jason found himself in the role of supporter. ''Truly, Miss Twickenham, when your father understands the circumstances, I'm sure he'll be grateful for Nathaniel's protection.''

''Throw a bucket of water on Mr. Shindler, Jacob,'' Nathaniel called to the stablehand. ''When he comes to, tell him he is to remain in his room until further word from Mr. Twickenham.''

''Wi' pleasure, Mr. Nathaniel. Wi' pleasure,'' the old man assured Mr. Denbigh with a toothless grin.

''Allow us to escort you back to the house, Miss Twickenham,'' Jason said kindly, offering his arm to the young lady. Tabitha seemed in a trance, a look of dismay on her face.

''Yes, of course,'' she agreed faintly. ''I must discuss this with Anne at once.''

———

''Could you not have just asked him to remove his hand?'' Georgina demanded again of her brother as they rode back to Greenbriar Manor.

"No, I could not! Would you prefer that I not come to your friend's defense? No gentleman would have left her to that excuse for a man."

"Jason did nothing. Are you suggesting *he* is not a gentleman?"

"Georgie! Of course I am not saying that!" Nathaniel protested.

Jason cleared his throat. "I would have acted if your brother had not," he assured his hostess. "Frankly, I was too surprised by the man's disgusting behavior to respond so quickly."

His irritation exacerbated by the three women's lack of enthusiasm for his chivalry, Nathaniel ground out, "I do not understand your behavior, Georgie!"

"Oh, Nathaniel, it is not that I do not appreciate your protection of Tabby. We are all grateful that you—well, *not* that you did so, but that you *wanted* to do so."

"That makes no sense at all," Nathaniel said in disgust.

"It is just that you do not know Mr. Twickenham. It is such an awkward time for him to visit."

"Why?" Jason asked.

Georgina realized she had revealed more than she intended. "Because—because you are both visiting and I had hoped to have a dinner party. I will have to invite Mr. Twickenham, and he is not very popular hereabout."

"It is your concern about your guest list that leaves you cool to my assisting Miss Twickenham?" Nathaniel asked incredulously.

"No! No, I did not mean that! But Mr. Twickenham does not care for Tabby and he can be monstrously cruel. He will not believe that it is not Tabby's fault."

The two men stared at her. "But we were both there, Georgina," Jason reminded her. "He will have the word of two gentlemen that Miss Twickenham did nothing to bring on such behavior.''

"Mr. Twickenham is not a gentleman. He is a cit,'' Georgina reminded them.

"Georgina Denbigh, Papa would reprimand you sharply if he heard you. He taught us to judge a man on his behavior, not his rank in society,'' Nathaniel reminded his sister.

"And I have done so,'' she responded. "You will see. He will descend upon us with much huffing, and he will side with Mr. Shindler. Tabby and Anne will suffer from your chivalrous act. Then you will understand why we reacted as we did.''

The two men gave up their argument. Nathaniel had an uneasy feeling that his sister might be right, but he could not allow a gently bred female to be subjected to such behavior. He would discuss it with his father.

Jason was amused. It was unusual for either his or his friend's behavior to be questioned. Nor did he often do the pretty to impressionable females. At least in one thing Nathaniel had been correct. Boredom was never a problem at Greenbriar Manor.

When the threesome arrived home, Jason discovered just how true his thoughts were. As they entered the front hall, his valet, Masterson, was anxiously awaiting him. "My lord, I have had news from London. My father is gravely ill. I would ask that you please allow me leave of absence.''

"Masterson, could you not have waited above stairs?'' Jason asked, embarrassed by his servant's public plea.

"Of course he could not, Jason. There is no need to stand on ceremony here,'' Georgina intervened. "Have you already packed to leave, Masterson?''

The man nodded, pathetically eager to be on his way.

Nathaniel and Georgina looked at Jason. "Well, of course you may go, Masterson," Jason said, before muttering under his breath, "though I'm not sure how I'll manage without you."

Georgina, having heard his second remark, sent her guest a reproving look.

Nathaniel asked, "Wilkins, have you ordered the carriage brought round?"

"Oh, no, sir. That's not necessary at all," the poor valet murmured, casting a worried look at his master.

"Nonsense. At least let our driver take you to Sheffield to the nearest posting house. You can catch the stagecoach there," Nathaniel explained. "Do you have enough funds?"

When the man was struck speechless in the face of such kindness, Georgina prodded Jason. "Give Masterson some additional blunt, Jason."

"What? Yes, of course. Here, Masterson," he said, taking several gold crowns from his pocket. "This should get you to London. If you need more upon your arrival, see Thompson," he added, naming his man of business.

"Thank you, my lord. You are most generous," Masterson said, moved almost to tears by his master's gesture.

The sound of a carriage at the front door ended their conversation and Masterson was bundled out the door by Wilkins.

"We hope all is well with your father, Masterson," Georgina called out to the little man as the carriage door closed behind him. His grateful look out the window was their last sight of him.

"What shall I do for a valet until Masterson returns?" Jason wondered out loud.

"Have you no feelings for that poor man?" Georgina asked.

"Of course I do, Georgie, but the fact remains that I have no knowledge of maintaining my wardrobe. Would you have me appear less than a gentleman?"

"No, Jason," Georgina said with a cheeky grin. "But a little less starch in your cravats might be nice."

"I'll have you know, my child, that my cravats are greatly admired in London."

"By all the fine ladies, I'm sure," Georgina teased.

"Is my daughter squabbling with our guest?" Mr. Denbigh asked in a wondering voice as he emerged from the library.

"No, Papa," Nathaniel assured him. "She is only instructing Jason in the proper attire for a gentleman."

"She is hoping to replace Masterson," Jason teased, his eyes on Georgina's rosy cheeks.

Embarrassed by such teasing, Georgina sought a distraction. "Papa, a terrible thing has happened."

"To Masterson?" Mr. Denbigh inquired in surprise.

"No. Well, of course, it is terrible about Masterson's father. That is the reason Masterson had to leave, but that is not what I meant," Georgina quickly explained. "Nathaniel had a fight with Mr. Shindler, and now I'm sure Mr. Twickenham will come, and he will be angry. He might even forbid Anne and Tabby to visit us."

Mr. Denbigh swung his gaze to his son, a frown on his face. "Nathaniel?"

"I will explain, Papa. May we discuss it in the library?" Nathaniel asked, aware of the butler standing by the door.

"Yes, of course. Wilkins, I believe we will be ready for luncheon in a half hour." After the butler had departed, Mr. Denbigh eyed the other two. "Georgie, I forbid you to become Jason's valet. You will have to find some other way to make your fortune."

"Yes, Papa," Georgina agreed with a grin, relieved at her father's teasing. Surely, if anyone could retrieve the situation, it would be her father.

Once the other two disappeared into the library, Georgina glanced at the tall man beside her. "I did not mean to criticize your appearance, Jason. You are always elegant in your dress. It has been a most upsetting day."

He smiled at her, then gently touched her cheek. "Yes, it has. First Mr. Shindler and then Masterson," Jason said, amused at her sudden docility.

"Yes, well, I will go change now."

"But what am I to do about a valet?" Jason demanded. "Is there a firm in Sheffield where I can hire one?"

"I doubt—wait! I have an idea!" Georgina exclaimed, eagerness lighting her brown eyes.

# Chapter Five

"You know where I can locate a valet to fill in until Masterson's return?" Jason asked in surprise.

"Not exactly," Georgina said, avoiding his eyes.

"Well?" Jason demanded when she did not continue.

"You see, one of our tenants was killed on the Peninsula, and I have taken an interest in the children. They have all been trained in service."

When she paused again, Jason prodded her. "One of them has been trained as a valet?"

"Not quite, but he would like to be," Georgina said swiftly, hoping to disarm her victim before he realized what she was suggesting. "He is a good boy. You will like him."

"What? You want me to take an untrained boy as my valet?" Jason demanded. "Do you know how long Masterson trained before I would even let him enter my bedroom?"

"Oh, pooh! What can be so very difficult about handing you your clothes? You are probably too concerned with your appearance, anyway."

"Georgina Denbigh, I should turn you over my knees and spank you!" Jason returned.

Undaunted by his threat, Georgina pleaded, "Please, Jason? It will only be for a few days, I'm sure, and it would mean so much to Albert if he could train under your expert tutelage.'' To accompany her words, she smiled meltingly at her companion.

"So now you're trying to turn me up sweet? Don't think you can get around me like that, Georgie,'' Jason warned even as he smiled. "Acting as my valet is quite complicated, and I doubt I know enough to teach anyone. Only someone of Masterson's caliber could do so.''

"But Wilkins once served Papa as valet. He could help Albert. And Papa and Nathaniel's valets could assist him. It would not be so bad, Jason. Please, won't you consider it?''

Georgina Denbigh made an enchanting picture in her blue riding jacket, her auburn hair cascading down her back in curls beneath her riding hat, and a winsome smile on her face. Despite his lack of faith in her plan, Jason found himself giving in. "I will consider it, Georgie, but I am making no promises.''

"Oh, thank you, Jason,'' she exclaimed as she threw her arms round his neck and kissed his cheek, just as she had done as a child when he had promised to teach her to swim. Then, she realized in shock that she'd acted like a child in front of him. Young ladies did not behave in such a manner.

Feeling awkward, she whisked herself away from him before Jason could respond, and turned to run up the stairs.

"I only promised to consider it, Georgie,'' he called after her, but he knew she had won the battle.

Jason remained standing in the hall, the memory of her lips on his cheek and her arms around his neck vivid in his mind. Her response was the same as the child he remembered, confirming his belief that she was not yet grown. The only difficulty was in the response she evoked in him. There was nothing brotherly about it.

When Georgina announced Albert's promotion at luncheon, Mr. Denbigh and Nathaniel were not as enthusiastic as she had hoped. In fact, Nathaniel burst into laughter. "You are assigning Albert to care for Jason?" he demanded once his chuckles had subsided.

"Yes, and I do not see what is so amusing. It will be a wonderful opportunity for Albert."

"I agree, but I was thinking about it more from Jason's viewpoint. I can't believe he will be comfortable with a mere untrained boy in Masterson's place," Nathaniel pointed out with a grin.

"Albert is not a child, and he will learn quickly. I think it is most admirable of Jason to agree." Georgina beamed at Albert's benefactor, who was regretting his submission to the young lady's wiles more and more.

"Yes, Jason, it is most generous of you. The *ton* will be amazed to learn of your consideration," Nathaniel taunted, ignoring Jason's fulminating glare.

"Nathaniel," his father cautioned, "I believe you have enough on your plate without teasing Jason. When Mr. Twickenham arrives, you may not feel quite so cheerful."

The grin was wiped from the younger Mr. Denbigh's face. "I still find it difficult to believe the man will take his manager's part. Does he care so little for his daughter?"

"You will see," Georgina predicted morosely.

"Georgie, were you able to ask Mrs. Hansen about working with me?" Mr. Denbigh asked.

"Yes, Papa. We settled that before the disaster occurred."

"I wish you will stop referring to my chivalrous rescue of Miss Twickenham in such terms," Nathaniel protested.

Georgina ignored her brother. Turning to her father, she

said, "She agreed to come over after breakfast in the morning and spend the day. At least she did before we realized Mr. Twickenham would be arriving soon. She was reluctant to accept payment until she realized it would provide a nest egg should she lose her position."

"Do you think Mr. Twickenham would go so far as to fire Mrs. Hansen?" Mr. Denbigh asked. "After all, from my understanding of the event, she was not involved."

"No, not exactly. But she has complained about Mr. Shindler before. And—and there are other points of disagreement."

Though Mr. Denbigh waited for a greater explanation, there was none forthcoming. Finally he said, "I will assure Mrs. Hansen that she is welcome to come here for a visit should it be necessary for her to leave Mr. Twickenham's residence."

"Thank you, Papa," Georgina said with a smile. If Mr. Twickenham fired Anne and she came to stay at Greenbriar Manor, Georgina's plan would not be necessary after all. But that would leave Tabby. Perhaps Anne working for her father would be the best solution, after all.

"When will Albert begin his duties?" Jason asked abruptly.

"I have not informed him of his good fortune yet. I'll do so after lunch, Jason. I'm sure he'll want to begin at once."

"When are you planning your dinner party?" Nathaniel asked. "Perhaps it will put Mr. Twickenham in a more generous mood."

"I will gladly include Mr. Twickenham, Nathaniel, because Tabby is my friend, but do not expect it to have any effect on the man. And it will ruin everyone else's evening," Georgina assured her brother.

"Georgie, the man may lack social skills, but he is still our neighbor," Mr. Denbigh reminded her.

"Perhaps he'll be so disgusted with Mr. Shindler, he'll decide to sell the estate," Nathaniel suggested. "If I promise to remain here to handle both estates, would you consider purchasing it, Papa?"

"But that would mean Tabby would move away! I don't want that to happen," Georgina exclaimed before her father could answer.

"Certainly we would consider such a move, Nathaniel, but I confess I would regret losing Mrs. Hansen and Tabitha as neighbors. They both seem admirable," Mr. Denbigh responded, pleasing both his children at once.

"Miss Twickenham will probably marry soon anyway, Georgie, so you might as well resign yourself to her departure. She is of that age," Nathaniel warned.

"And what age is that?" Georgina asked stiffly.

"Your brother means if she does not marry soon, she will be considered on the shelf," Jason put in, amused at Georgina's irritation.

"I do not think it proper or gentlemanly to discuss a lady's age," Georgina pointed out.

Nathaniel frowned at his sister. "Miss Twickenham cannot be much older than you." He turned to his father. "Is Georgina going to be presented?"

"Surely she is too young," Jason protested involuntarily.

"I have discussed that subject with Georgie several times, Nathaniel, but each time she has put me off. I suppose I have been lax in the matter. But like Jason," Mr. Denbigh acknowledged with a sigh, "I always consider her too young. And besides, Georgie keeps me so comfortable, it is too tempting to agree with her."

"Yes, but we don't want to wait until she is considered

an ape-leader. People will think there is something wrong with her.''

''I think you are exaggerating the seriousness of the situation, Nathaniel,'' Jason suggested.

''I do not want a season!'' Georgina protested, drawing all eyes.

Nathaniel ignored his sister's outburst. ''I have been neglectful to both of you, Papa. I am glad I have been reminded of my duties. We shall present Georgie this spring in London.''

''*You* have nothing to say about my future, Nathaniel!'' Georgina exclaimed. ''That is for Papa to decide, not you.''

''She does have a point, son. While I am grateful for your presence, I am still capable of managing my own household.'' Before Georgina could breathe a sigh of relief, however, her father added, ''But we must consider your future, Georgie. Your brother is right.''

Georgina knew better than to argue with her father in front of the others, but she had no intention of being hauled off to the marriage mart in London.

As soon as the meal ended, Georgina left the men in the library and headed for the kitchen. Before she could reach the stairs, however, she was halted by Jason.

''Georgina!'' he called from the hallway.

She swung around but did not retrace her steps.

''I apologize if anything I said at luncheon caused you any distress,'' he said, smiling down at her.

''Thank you, Jason, but it was my brother, not you, who is bent on causing difficulties.''

''Have you no desire to be presented? I agree that you are perhaps too young at the moment, but it is most young women's dream,'' Jason said in surprise.

''But it is not mine. They are shown off for the highest

bidder, as you well know, and exposed to society's cruelties.''

Jason was astounded by her reaction. ''Georgina, surely you realize you are exaggerating. What has caused you to be so prejudiced against London society?''

''Tabby's experience does not indicate an exaggeration.''

Jason rushed to reassure her. ''You need have no fears, Georgie. You are a beautiful young woman. You will be greatly admired,'' he said with the sort of smile he might use to comfort a child.

''Thank you, Jason, but I believe I would prefer to remain in the country.''

He reached out a finger to flick the soft skin of her cheek. ''When you are a little older, you will change your mind, Georgie.'' He chuckled indulgently. ''Once your thoughts have turned from Chester and your horses, you will see the advantage of a London season.''

''Why do you persist in seeing me as a child?'' Georgina demanded. ''I am an adult now, and I do not want to go to London!'' Much to Jason's surprise, tears filled her brown eyes and the young lady turned and fled up the stairs, leaving him staring after her in dismay.

Her mission below stairs was forgotten. Throwing herself across her bed, Georgina sobbed into her pillow without knowing the reason for her anguish.

She did not want to go to London. She also did not want Jason to see her as a child. And she refused to ask herself why his view of her should be so important. Instead, she chastised herself for behaving so childishly just now, only reinforcing his opinion. From now on, she vowed, she would show Jason just how mature and adult she could be!

When Anne and Tabitha arrived at Greenbriar Manor the next morning, Georgina met them in the front parlor. "Have you heard from Mr. Twickenham?" she asked at once.

"No, not yet," Anne replied. "I wrote him a note and sent it by messenger yesterday, but I'm sure he will come in person."

"And will he stop you from visiting us?" Georgina asked.

"I will run away if he does!" Tabitha exclaimed, tears in her eyes.

As she was comforted by Anne and Georgina, none of the ladies heard Mr. Denbigh enter the parlor. "Is something amiss?" he asked.

Anne jumped to her feet. "Oh, no, Mr. Denbigh. That is, Tabitha is concerned about her father's reaction to—to the problem with Mr. Shindler. That is all."

"I offer my apologies for whatever distress my son has caused you, but he could not allow that creature to manhandle Miss Twickenham."

"No, of course not. I was not suggesting—"

"Nathaniel was wonderful!" Tabitha assured the older Mr. Denbigh. "He was ever so b-brave." She carried her lacy handkerchief to her face. "But I am such a coward."

Even as Anne comforted her charge, she smiled ruefully at Mr. Denbigh. "Tabitha is overwrought, Mr. Denbigh. We should have remained at home, but I promised Georgie I would come today to work on the drawings for your book. However, if you would prefer that we postpone our work until after everything is settled, I will understand."

"I have been looking forward to our working together today if you feel ready to do so," Mr. Denbigh assured her.

With a relieved nod, Anne asked, "Tabitha, will you be all right with Georgie?"

"Of course, Anne. I will be fine," that young lady said bravely, only sniffing twice.

As soon as the two older adults had left the room, Georgie and Tabby collapsed on the sofa. "What are we going to do?" Tabitha demanded of her friend.

"I don't know, Tabby. It depends on your father's reaction. Perhaps he will surprise us."

"Ha! He will be as beastly as ever!"

After a glum pause, Georgina jumped to her feet. "Moping will not help us. We must just await his arrival. Will you help me with the reader I am preparing?"

Though Tabitha's response was less than enthusiastic, Georgina rang for Wilkins and requested Molly to bring down her papers. Soon the two young ladies were discussing the best path for the hero of Georgina's story, *Fusby the Cat*.

She had begun a small class for the children of the servants and farm families the year before when she realized how little schooling the children received.

One of the difficulties Georgina discovered was the lack of materials or interesting stories for her young readers. She conceived the idea of writing her own only recently and *Fusby* was the result. She involved Tabitha in the story to help her forget her own difficulties.

"But Georgie, cats do not swim!" Tabitha protested, as she pointed to what her friend had written.

Nathaniel and Jason, entering at that moment, looked at each other in surprise.

"I was about to ask if we might join you for the tea Wilkins is bringing, but it appears we are interrupting a most serious discussion," Nathaniel said in amusement, causing both young ladies to jump.

Sure she was presenting Jason another example of her childishness, Georgina hastened to gather up her papers as she welcomed the two gentlemen. "Of course you may join us for tea. I had not realized the time."

"You must have spent an enjoyable morning," Jason commented cautiously. He didn't want to cause little Georgie any more distress, though he wasn't sure how he had done so yesterday.

"Oh, yes, it is always amusing to work on Georgie's bo—"

"Never mind, Tabby!" Georgina hastened to interrupt. She had no intention of exposing *Fusby the Cat* to one who already considered her a child.

"Georgie's what?" Nathaniel questioned Tabitha, ignoring his sister's efforts to silence her friend.

Since Tabitha had already identified Nathaniel as her knight in shining armor, she could never refuse to tell him anything. "Georgie's book. She is preparing a story book for the children."

"What children?" Nathaniel demanded. "What are you up to, Georgie, and does Papa know?"

"Of course he knows and approves," Georgina stiffly replied. "And it is none of your business." She had not yet forgiven her brother for his remarks about a London season.

"Oh, Georgie, you should not be so modest. She is teaching all the children to read. She is very good at it," Tabitha boasted.

"That is admirable, Georgie," Nathaniel agreed.

Jason nodded but said nothing. Georgie didn't seem happy with their praise, and he didn't want to put a foot wrong again.

Fortunately, in Georgina's opinion, their conversation was interrupted by the arrival of the tea tray. When they had all been served, Nathaniel reintroduced the young women's original subject of conversation. "Has your father communicated with you about yesterday, Miss Twickenham?"

Tabitha ducked her head, trying to hide her dismay from the gentlemen. "Not yet."

"I promise you that I will explain. I am sure once your father has heard the events, he will understand and approve of your actions," Nathaniel said, his eyes trained on the young lady.

"Thank you, sir," Tabitha whispered. In her heart, she did not believe anything Nathaniel said could soften her father's reaction, but she appreciated his offer.

"Would you two care to join us on a ride around the estate?" Nathaniel asked, hoping to relieve any possible embarrassment.

"That would be wonderful," Tabitha agreed, blushing, until she remembered she was not dressed for riding. "But I did not bring my riding habit with me."

"We can take a buggy," Nathaniel offered, ignoring his friend's grimace.

"Why don't you take Tabitha with you?" Georgie offered. "I have a lot of chores to do that would bore her." After all, grown up ladies didn't waste their days away riding with the gentlemen.

"But I wanted you to bring me up to date on the families around the estate," Nathaniel said.

"Tabby can do that as well as I. She often accompanies me when I make my rounds. You do not mind, do you, Tabby?"

That young lady's smile provided the answer to Georgina's question and she nodded to her brother. Now Tabby and Nathaniel would be together, and at the same time she would be able to convince Jason of her maturity, though she thought with longing of being outdoors.

"Surely you can postpone whatever chores you have to go with us, Georgina," Jason suggested.

Georgina decided he must see her work as unimportant and frowned fiercely at him, causing Jason to wonder what he had done now. "No, I cannot. I am preparing some surprises for the children at Christmas, which will soon be upon us." The eight-year-old Georgina would have ended her remark by sticking out her tongue, but she, of course, was too mature for such a reaction.

"Perhaps another time," Jason muttered. Georgina suddenly seemed very touchy, unlike her usual open and friendly self. He regretted the change.

"We will hold luncheon until your return, so you'd best be off right away," Georgina said, standing to force the other three out the door.

Nathaniel, ignoring the stiffness between his sister and friend, said with a smile, "We may be several hours."

"That's all right," Georgina assured him. "I have a great deal to do, and you know Papa will never notice the time when he is working on his beloved book."

With only a few more attempts, Georgina sped the three on their way and sank back onto the sofa with a sigh. Being an adult seemed so tiresome this morning.

# Chapter Six

For the next several days, Anne and Tabitha traveled each morning to Greenbriar Manor for Anne to assist Mr. Denbigh in his work. Tabitha visited with Georgina and then accompanied the two men about the estate as Nathaniel familiarized himself with his home once more.

Georgina, having finished the story of *Fusby the Cat* to her satisfaction, was now copying his adventure over and over again, making a book, with illustrations, for each of her students. Though she occasionally paused to sigh and look longingly out the window, she always returned to her task.

She would have had to stay inside even without Jason's presence, she reminded herself. There was too much to do. Along with the book, she was knitting mittens for the children. Everywhere she went, she took her bag of yarn.

On the fourth day, the three returned early from their daily excursion and discovered Georgina knitting in the parlor.

"You should have come with us," Nathaniel said as they entered. "It is a beautiful, crisp day outside."

Georgina replied, "Jackson says it will snow this evening."

"Ah, then it is sure to do so. Our head groom is never

wrong about the weather," Nathaniel assured the others as he pulled out a chair by the fire for Tabitha.

"And does he bring you a weather report each day?" Jason asked blandly. He was irritated and a bit puzzled by Georgina's refusal to budge from the front parlor.

"No, but I wanted to check on Dumpling, my mare. She is to foal in a few days," Georgina informed him.

"Dumpling?" Jason asked in surprise. "That is an unusual name for a young lady's steed."

Georgina kept her head high even though her cheeks were red. "She is the color of a dumpling and rather round, but she is very fast."

"That is not a name to lend confidence in her speed," Jason said with a laugh.

Dropping her eyes, Georgina returned her attention to her knitting. Why had she called her horse such a ridiculous name? He still thought her childish, she realized, despite her self-imposed imprisonment in the parlor.

"I told Wilkins to move up luncheon since we are back early, Georgie," Nathaniel said. "I hope it will not discommode Papa and Mrs. Hansen."

"I doubt they will even notice the difference. I believe Anne is as enthusiastic about their project as Papa."

Georgina managed a small self-satisfied smile, happy that that part of her plan was working.

"I am fortunate Tabitha has accompanied me these last few days. She is quite knowledgeable about our tenants," Nathaniel commented.

"That is because Georgie has taught me a lot about country life, and I have enjoyed our rides very much, Nathaniel," Tabitha said, her cheeks pink.

Georgina's eyebrows rose. "Have we discarded the formalities, then?"

Nathaniel said carelessly, "It seemed silly when we have

been spending so much time together. After all, you and Tabitha are close friends.''

"True," Georgina agreed, noting her friend's blush.

"Tabitha has even agreed to discard my title, just as you have done," Jason added, but he did not seem nearly as pleased as the other two.

"Well, that is—" Georgina's words were halted by a loud pounding on the front door. Tabitha and Georgina exchanged apprehensive looks.

The butler opened the parlor door. "Mr. Twickenham has called, Miss Georgina."

"Thank you, Wilkins. You may show him in."

Georgina continued with her knitting, though she was afraid she might have to undo her work later. Tabitha sat white-faced, waiting for her father's entrance.

A large, heavy-set man entered the room, his red face and bulbous nose clashing with the yellow of his waistcoat and bottle-green jacket. "Good day, Miss Denbigh, Tabitha," he growled, staring at the two gentlemen.

"Good day, Mr. Twickenham. May I present to you my brother, Mr. Denbigh, and his friend, Lord Chesterton," Georgina said calmly. When the men had greeted each other, she said, "Won't you be seated? I'll have Wilkins bring a fresh pot of tea to warm you. The weather is quite brisk today."

"Nay, I'll not take tea. I've come to collect my daughter and Mrs. Hansen."

"But, Papa—" Tabitha began.

"Mr. Twickenham—" Nathaniel interrupted, and then stopped with a bow to the young lady. "I beg your pardon, Tabitha, but I believe I should speak to your father before your departure."

Mr. Twickenham, surprised, turned to stare first at Nathaniel and then at his daughter. "Well, I never expected you to bring it off, Tabitha, my girl. You've caught your-self the squire's son, have you? Not as good as a title, but I didn't expect this much after that mess in London." Mr. Twickenham's booming voice seemed to echo in the re-sulting silence.

Tabitha hid her face in mortification and Nathaniel's cheeks flamed as he hurriedly said, "I wanted to speak to you about the incident with Mr. Shindler, sir."

"You mean you don't intend to marry my daughter?" the man demanded in irritation.

"If you will excuse us, I will take Tabitha upstairs to—to wash for luncheon. Will you join us, Mr. Twicken-ham?" Georgina asked in a rush.

"Nay, I want to get this matter with Shindler settled. I'll take my womenfolk home now."

"Mr. Twickenham," Jason interrupted for the first time, all the authority of his title in his voice. "Mr. Denbigh and I have some information regarding Mr. Shindler that you should hear, and it is a half-hour drive to your home. Surely it would be best to allow the ladies to dine before you carry them off?"

Despite himself, Mr. Twickenham allowed his awe of a title to persuade him. "Very well. We leave immediately after luncheon," he growled at his daughter, who refused to raise her gaze from the floor.

Without another word, Georgina pulled her friend from the room, shutting the door behind them. Wilkins emerged from his pantry and awaited his orders.

"Wilkins, Mr. Twickenham will be joining us for lun-cheon." Georgina waited until the butler had left before saying, "Tabby, you go up to my room. Ask Molly to bring you a cup of tea. I must speak to Papa and Anne."

Tabitha gulped, nodded in gratitude, and scurried up the stairs. Georgina rushed down the hall to the library.

After a brief knock, she entered the room where her father and Anne were sitting with their heads together, studying a drawing.

Mr. Denbigh looked up reluctantly. "Hello, my dear. Is it luncheon already?"

"In a few minutes, Papa. But we will have an additional guest. Mr. Twickenham has arrived."

"Oh, dear," Anne muttered, her eyes widening.

"Is he in an unpleasant mood?" her father asked with a twinkle in his eye. He knew Georgina always considered the man to be in such a mood.

"Yes. But he has embarrassed Tabitha beyond words by assuming Nathaniel wished to offer for her when he said he wanted to talk to him about Mr. Shindler," Georgina explained.

"Poor Tabby. She must be horrified," Anne said. "I must go to her at once."

"She has retreated to my room. Papa, could you go to the parlor? I am afraid Nathaniel will lose his temper, and Mr. Twickenham will forbid Anne and Tabby to visit."

"Of course, child," Mr. Denbigh said, rising from the sofa. "You take Anne upstairs, and I'll join the others."

"Thank you, Papa," Georgina said, hugging her father even as she noted the dismissal of formality between himself and Mrs. Hansen.

"Alistair, you will be careful, won't you? He is a big man and has a terrible temper," Anne added quietly.

Though Mr. Denbigh was fairly tall, he had a lean frame in comparison to Mr. Twickenham's massive proportions. He smiled in response. "I promise not to challenge him to a duel, my dear. You go upstairs with Georgie."

The two women followed Mr. Denbigh down the hall. After he entered the parlor, pulling the door to behind him, they looked at each other.

"I wish we could listen at the door," Georgina whispered, "but I'm afraid we would be caught. Shall we see how poor Tabby is faring?"

Anne nodded and the two tiptoed up the stairs. They found that young lady sipping a cup of tea by the window, her cheeks now pale.

"Tabby, are you all right?" Anne asked lovingly.

"Oh, Anne!" Tabitha exclaimed, rising to be enfolded in her companion's arms. "It was horrible. Papa thought . . . Nathaniel has no intention of . . . oh, I could die!"

"I'm sure Nathaniel will not hold your father's words against you, child. It was a mistake, that's all."

Raising her head, Tabitha said, "But you know Papa will be doubly angry now. He considers me less than useless. He will side with Mr. Shindler and I will be in disgrace."

"Papa has gone to the parlor to help convince Mr. Twickenham, Tabby. You may rely on him."

"Yes," Anne agreed with Georgina. "We may count on Alistair's good judgment, Tabby. Let us keep our fingers crossed that he is able to convince your father."

———

Mr. Denbigh slipped into the parlor in time to hear Mr. Twickenham's response to his son's explanation of the events involving Tabitha and Mr. Shindler.

"My daughter had no business interfering in Shindler's way of handling things. He knows his job and he answers to me, not my daughter."

"Mr. Twickenham," Nathaniel protested, "I have explained that the man grabbed your daughter's arm. Surely you will not countenance such disrespect. Besides, he was drunk!"

"A little whiskey to warm him on a cold day, that's all. The girl gets hysterical. She had no call to bother him."

"Perhaps," Mr. Denbigh interrupted calmly, "Nathaniel has already explained that she did so at his request. My son is greatly interested in your estate and was dismayed to discover the deterioration Mr. Shindler has allowed."

Mr. Twickenham turned around to stare at his host. "It's none of his nor your business what happens on my estate. I'll thank you to tend to your own affairs and leave mine alone."

"And your daughter?" Nathaniel demanded. "It is any gentleman's business if she is insulted in my presence. Do you care nothing for your daughter's welfare?"

With all three men staring at him, Mr. Twickenham seemed to bite back his first response. Finally, he said, "Girl's useless. She should've stayed in the house."

Nathaniel turned his back on the man, unable to face him and remain calm. Mr. Denbigh looked at his son and then Mr. Twickenham before saying, "Please be seated, sir. I believe we have something to discuss."

After a hard stare at his host, Mr. Twickenham settled his large frame into a delicate chair. "Don't see that we do. Shindler is my manager. There's nothing more to it."

Mr. Denbigh placed a hand on his son's shoulder and guided him to a seat on the sofa, nodding for Jason to join him. Then he sat down in a chair close to Mr. Twickenham.

"Sir, my son has long had an interest in your estate. I was slow to act after Mr. Buxton's death and you purchased it before I could do so. But, over the past few months, it has become clear that you are a city man and have little liking for the land. I wondered if you would consider selling it to us."

Mr. Twickenham's small eyes narrowed, and he stared first at Mr. Denbigh and then his son. "It's true I don't have much interest in land,'' he said slowly, ''but I needed a place for my daughter to live, out of the way. She don't care for London.''

No one made any comment, waiting for the man to continue.

''We might could strike a deal,'' Mr. Twickenham said, a gleam in his eye.

''Name your price,'' Nathaniel said eagerly, and his father shook his head. The cit was a skilled negotiator.

''Aye, my price. Well, young fellow, it may be too high for you to pay, but I'll name it. My price is my daughter.''

Nathaniel stared blankly at the man, but Jason and Mr. Denbigh exchanged looks. Mr. Denbigh took pity on his son's incomprehension. ''Perhaps you would explain further, Mr. Twickenham.''

''Well, see now, here I am with a daughter who needs a husband, and here you are wanting my land. Seems to me the answer is to make the land her dowry. You marry her and you get the land. It's as simple as that,'' he said, smugly crossing his arms and waiting for Nathaniel's response.

''That—that is impossible,'' Nathaniel exclaimed, jumping up from the sofa and striding across the room to stare out the window. He spun around then to say, ''Miss Twickenham may have no interest in marrying me.''

''Don't matter. She'll do as she's told. I don't hold with disobedient children.'' Mr. Twickenham kept his eyes on Nathaniel. ''She's not ill featured, you know.''

''I never meant to imply she was,'' the young man replied, flustered.

''It's not such a bad bargain—a pretty wife and an estate the size of mine. And you could take care of that neglect you think you see,'' Mr. Twickenham added.

''We appreciate the offer, sir,'' Mr. Denbigh said, his

eyes on his son, "and should my son have an interest in it, we will contact you."

"Best do so in a hurry. I may change my mind."

"I assure you—" Mr. Denbigh started in irritation, but his son interrupted.

"I accept your offer," Nathaniel said harshly, "if Miss Twickenham does not dislike it."

"I told you she'd not have a choice," the man said, rubbing his hands together gleefully.

"Nathaniel! You must be sure—" Mr. Denbigh began, and Jason rose from the sofa to stride to his friend's side.

But Nathaniel refused to listen to words of caution. "I know what I am doing, Papa, Jason. Miss Twickenham is a pleasant young lady. I have been on the town for a number of years and have discovered no one I want to marry, so I think she will suit me very well." He paused and his eyes took on a new light as he added, "You know I have always wanted the land. It means a great deal to me."

After studying his son for several minutes, Mr. Denbigh nodded in agreement. "I would prefer you not enter marriage in this manner, but you have the right to make your own decision."

"Your son is a smart man. Women can be found aplenty, but a good estate is hard to come by," Mr. Twickenham assured Mr. Denbigh. "Well, this is a good day's work. I never thought I'd rid myself of two problems in one day," he said.

"There is only one condition," Nathaniel said, interrupting Mr. Twickenham's self-congratulations.

"Condition?" the man demanded.

"I must be sure that Miss Twickenham is not averse to our marriage. I would like to ask for her hand in marriage before you talk to her."

"Nay, I know how to handle the girl. I'll make sure

she don't harbor any of them romantical notions girls get. You leave it to me," Mr. Twickenham said hastily.

"No." There was no softness in Nathaniel's answer. "I must speak with her, alone, before the agreement is made."

"I believe my son's request is not unreasonable," Mr. Denbigh added.

Mr. Twickenham's frustration was visible, but he had little choice. He had even less confidence that his daughter would make a wise decision. "Very well," he agreed dolefully. "But you are making a mistake. It would be better to leave the girl to me."

Jason asked, "Shall I ask Wilkins to call Miss Twickenham to the library?"

"Yes, thank you, Jason," Nathaniel said gratefully. "I'll await her there."

"You tell her that her pa expects her to accept!" Mr. Twickenham called out as the two younger men left the room.

———

All three women came down in response to Wilkins's message. Jason was waiting for them at the foot of the stairs, reluctant to reenter the parlor.

"Jason, why is Tabby to go to the library? Is her father there?" Georgina demanded.

"No, only Nathaniel is in the library," he answered.

"Why Nathaniel? What does he have to say to Tabby?" Georgina asked before her eyes widened. There was only one thing she could think of that would require her brother to speak to her friend in private. "What is going on?" she asked in a small voice.

Tabitha stood white-faced, her eyes focused on Jason, waiting for his response.

"Georgina, you must not ask me that. Tabitha and Nathaniel will explain."

Tabitha left the others and turned back down the hall to the library. They watched as she paused outside the door to stare back at her friends before opening the door and disappearing from view.

"My lord, surely you can tell us what is going on?" Anne asked.

With a grimace, Jason said quietly, "Nathaniel has offered for Tabitha and Mr. Twickenham has given the estate as a dowry."

The two women gasped. "Is Tabitha willing?" Georgina asked in surprise.

"It does not matter," Anne said with a frown. "Tabby must accept. Her father will leave her no choice."

The three stood in silence, wondering what was taking place in the library. Finally, Jason said, "Shall we join the others in the parlor?"

With a reluctant nod, the two ladies preceded him across the hall.

———

Nathaniel was standing with his back to the door as Tabitha entered the library. She wanted to turn and run before he saw her, but whatever was about to happen, she knew she had little choice.

"Nathaniel?" she murmured as she closed the door behind her.

"Ah, Tabitha, I did not hear you enter." Nathaniel gestured toward the sofa, and she moved over to sit down before her shaky limbs betrayed her.

He joined her there but was unable to meet her eyes. Staring across the room, he said, "My father asked to purchase your father's estate since it appeared he has little interest in farming.'' He paused but Tabitha said nothing, only biting her lip.

Raising his eyes, Nathaniel stared at the young woman in compassion. Quietly he said, ''Your father offered the estate as your dowry if I would marry you.''

Tabitha swung her face away and covered it with her hands, muttering, ''I'm sorry,'' through her fingers.

''It is done every day, Tabitha. You have nothing to be ashamed of, though it is not usually so—so abrupt,'' Nathaniel assured her. When she continued to hide her face, he reached warm fingers to encase hers and pull them away. ''You must not be embarrassed. I have told your father I will accept his offer, but I wanted to be sure—that is, do you think you could enter into such a marriage?''

Tabitha understood very well what Nathaniel Denbigh was offering. Her father was a businessman. He had found a market in which to sell his daughter. She nodded in agreement, but her heart was breaking. Her hidden dream of Nathaniel Denbigh courting her, loving her, was shattered.

''You are agreeable to our marriage? I will withdraw my offer if you do not think you will be happy as my wife.'' When there was no more response, he added, ''But we seem to deal together well. And you enjoy country life, and work well with the tenants. I think our marriage will be a good one.''

''Yes, sir,'' Tabitha answered, her eyes downcast. She had been taught not to express her feelings or opinion. She knew better than to do so now.

Nathaniel frowned, puzzled by her response. Their situation was a little embarrassing, of course, but he had hoped for at least some enthusiasm from his future bride. After all, he was considered a good catch in London and he was quite fond of her.

''Tabitha?''

She raised her blue eyes, blinking away the moisture that would betray her. ''Yes, I am pleased to accept your offer,'' she whispered.

''Then, shall we inform our fathers?'' Nathaniel asked. They rose and he offered her his arm.

# Chapter Seven

Georgina sat beside the fire in her room, her knitting occupying her hands, thoughts of the afternoon occupying her mind. She had not expected Mr. Twickenham to aid her in her schemes. It was the first time they had been of like minds, she was sure. It pleased her that Tabitha was going to be her sister-in-law. But the look on Tabitha's face as Nathaniel announced their betrothal caused her concern.

Tabitha was infatuated with Nathaniel, and he considered their marriage a business arrangement. Could her friend be happy with such an arrangement?

A shout rang through the house, startling Georgina from her reflections. Throwing her knitting on the floor, she ran from her room in time to see several servants race toward the guest room three doors down from hers. Knowing that was Jason's room, Georgina followed in their footsteps.

Loud voices drew everyone closer.

"You oaf! That water was like ice! You're supposed to heat it first!"

Georgina recognized Jason's cultured tones even at their most strident. "Give me my wrap!"

"Sorry, sir, I mean, my lord! I forgot! See, it's this way. I was ironing them necktie things when you wanted a bath in the middle of the day," Albert said, his words underlying his opinion of such an activity, "and I got all nervous and I was hurryin' to make sure I pleased you and—''

"Enough!" Jason snapped.

"Is everything all right?" Georgina called, standing to one side of the open door after dismissing the gaping servants.

"Georgie! Close the door, you muttonhead!" The door was slammed shut in time, Georgina hoped, to muffle the giggles she was no longer able to hold back. It reopened before she could move away. Albert stuck his head out into the hall and whispered, "His Lordship would like to talk to you in half an hour in the parlor, please, Miss Georgie."

"All right, Albert. Are you all right?" she whispered.

"Why, o' course, Miss Georgie. The master here is all bark and no bite. He don't mean no harm." Albert gave her a cheeky grin and ducked back into the room just as Jason roared again.

Georgina hurried back to her room. She would have to hasten her own toilette if she was to meet Jason in half an hour. She was sure he wanted to complain about Albert. But at least he had distracted her from her concerns.

———

When Georgina reached the parlor, she discovered Jason had not yet descended. She settled into a wing chair before the brightly burning fire and took out her ever-present knitting from the bag.

She did not have to wait long for company to arrive, but it was her brother rather than Jason who joined her.

"Good evening, sister," Nathaniel said as he moved to the warmth of the fire. "I think Jackson is right again in his forecast. Snow is beginning to fall."

Georgina had no interest in the snow outdoors. She wanted to ask Nathaniel about his feelings for Tabitha but knew he would not answer. "Yes, Jackson is always right," she agreed absently, keeping her eyes on her knitting.

For several minutes, the only noises were the clicking of Georgina's needles and the crunching of the burning wood. Finally, as if he could bear the silence no longer, Nathaniel burst out, "What do you think of today's events?"

Georgina considered and rejected several responses before saying, "I was surprised."

Nathaniel swung around to face her. "Are you not pleased to have Tabitha as your new sister-in-law?"

"I am delighted . . . if you are both happy."

"What are you saying, Georgie? Do you think I forced her into this marriage? I assure you I did not—"

"Georgie? I cannot bear—" Jason said as he entered the parlor, coming to an abrupt halt when he realized his audience was larger than he expected.

Georgina welcomed the interruption. "What is the matter, Jason?"

Jason looked at the faces of the two people before him and said, "Do the two of you wish to speak privately? I could—"

"No!" Georgina assured him.

"It appears that my little sister is not in favor of my coming marriage," Nathaniel announced to Jason.

"I did not say that, Nathaniel. You are placing a different meaning upon my words." Georgina's knitting sped up as her agitation increased.

"If you are pleased, Nathaniel, that is what is important."

Jason's calm statement brought a frown to Nathaniel's face, and Georgina concentrated on her knitting.

"Well, of course, I am pleased with the arrangement.

Mr. Buxton's estate is—was a magnificent property. I have always wanted it.''

Georgina's head snapped up. "Is that all this arrangement means to you? A piece of property? What about Tabitha?''

When Nathaniel had no response for his sister, his friend stepped in. "Marriages have been thus arranged since forever, Georgie. I am sure your friend understands.''

Georgina *wasn't* sure, but she had already said too much. She turned her attention back to her knitting.

The entrance of Mr. Denbigh distracted the two younger men.

He strolled over to sit down on the sofa. "How is your knitting project, Georgie?''

"Fine, Papa.''

"Good. I am proud of your activities on behalf of our people. Have you completed plans for the Christmas party for the children?''

"Yes, Papa. Mrs. Wilkins and I have arranged everything.''

"Fine. Well, Jason, do you enjoy the snow? It looks like everything will be covered long before morning.'' As Mr. Denbigh looked at his guest for a response, his eyes narrowed and he frowned.

"Yes, sir, I—is anything amiss?'' Jason asked as he noticed Mr. Denbigh's distraction.

"No, of course not, my boy. I just—that is, is there something different about your cravat this evening? I don't believe I've ever seen that particular style.''

Jason gave a disgusted look at the only female occupant of the room. "I'm sure you have not, sir. As you know, my valet had to leave and Georgie offered me the services of one of your servants. He is, uh, untrained in the art of maintaining a gentleman's wardrobe.''

"Oh, yes, I remember," Mr. Denbigh said, trying to hide a smile.

"I tried to arrive early to dinner to explain my difficulties to Georgie, but Nathaniel came down before me and I have been unable to speak with her concerning the matter."

"Ah. Then that was not the subject under discussion when I arrived?" Mr. Denbigh asked, looking at the three young people, all of whom dropped their eyes.

"No, Papa," Nathaniel finally said. "We were discussing my upcoming marriage."

"I hope you wished your brother happy, my dear?" Mr. Denbigh asked his daughter.

"Of course, I wish both of you happiness," Georgina said truthfully.

"Dinner is served, sir," Wilkins said, stepping into the parlor.

"Thank you, Wilkins," Mr. Denbigh said with a smile as he offered his arm to his daughter. "Perfect timing, eh, my dear?" After Georgina rose to take his arm, he whispered, "We'll discuss the upcoming nuptials another time, Georgina."

She looked up into her father's brown eyes so like her own and sighed deeply. Of course, she should have known her father would understand her difficulty.

---

The engagement and the as yet unscheduled marriage were not mentioned at the dinner table. Mr. Denbigh, Georgina and Jason discussed a variety of subjects while Nathaniel only gave an occasional absentminded comment. After dinner, Mr. Denbigh returned to his beloved studies and Georgina joined the two young gentlemen in the parlor. As she took her knitting from the bag, Jason asked, "Georgina, just what are you knitting so industriously?"

"Mittens for the children."

"The children? You mean all the children on the estate?" he repeated, astounded.

Georgina looked up in surprise. "Why, yes. For Christmas, you know," she added in explanation.

Before Jason could respond, Wilkins appeared at the door. "Miss Georgie, Jackson sent word. It's your mare."

All thought of anything but her beloved horse flew from Georgina's mind. "Send for Molly to bring my—" She stopped as Molly appeared beside the butler, her mistress's warm cloak, gloves, and boots in her hands.

"I sent for her already, Miss Georgie," Wilkins said, justifiably proud of his initiative. "I knew you'd be going to the stables."

"Thank you, Wilkins. Come to the morning room and help me don my boots, please, Molly," Georgina requested as she ran down the hall.

"Surely your sister is not going out in this storm?" Jason asked, startled by Georgina's behavior.

"Yes, and I suppose that means I should accompany her. Papa would not let her go alone and he is at work," Nathaniel said with a sigh. "Remain here by the fire, Jason. There is no need for both of us to freeze this evening."

Jason stood still, thinking. He heard movement in the hall and discovered Georgina, her auburn hair covered by the deep blue wool hood of her cloak. "Georgie? Surely your head groom can care for your mare? It is cold outside and no place for a child."

Georgina stared at him. Finally, she said, "I must be there to help Dumpling. It is not going to be an easy delivery." Without another word, she ran down the back stairs.

Jason waited a moment, a frown on his face, before he

too went upstairs to bundle up. He could not remain by the warm hearth while his friend and Georgina spent the evening in the cold.

———

Jason closed the door of the barn behind him, shutting out the near blizzard that had impeded his progress to the stables. After leaning against the door to catch his breath, he pulled his multi-layered cape tightly around him and moved down the row of stalls toward the lanterns' glow.

Georgina glanced up as she felt more than saw another presence. All her energies were concentrated on her beloved mare. She held its head in her lap, stroking the arched neck and crooning to it. Nathaniel, standing beside the door to the box stall, greeted his friend.

"You should have stayed inside where it is warm, Jason. There is nothing you can do here."

"I thought I could at least offer my support. Is it a difficult birth?"

"Jackson is trying to turn the colt." A sudden squeal from the mare drew everyone's attention. Several men were gathered around the animal, assisting the grey-haired man whom Jason took to be Jackson.

Jason turned his eyes from the men to the young woman sitting in the straw comforting her mare. The soft yellow glow of the lanterns created an aureole of light around her hair, giving it the glow of a warm fire. Her fingers were shaking from the cold, but she constantly moved them over the greyish-white head in her lap. She cared nothing for the damage done to her gown or cloak. Her eyes were full of love for the animal.

Over an hour later, Jackson successfully attended the delivery of Dumpling's foal, a trembling filly whose first attempts to stand brought relieved laughter from those gathered around her.

Jason moved into the stall to assist Georgina to her feet as Jackson did the same for Dumpling.

"I seem to be incapable of standing," Georgina said with a shaky laugh as she leaned against Jason's large frame.

"You remained seated too long. I will support you until you recover," he said, his nose inhaling the fresh scent of her hair.

"Oh, Jason, isn't she beautiful?" Georgina asked, her eyes on the newborn foal.

"Yes, she is, Georgie," he agreed, his arms involuntarily tightening against her.

"I—I am able to stand now," Georgina said, pulling away from him self-consciously. It had been all too comfortable there in his arms. She moved over to hug Dumpling's neck. "Good girl. You have a beautiful new baby."

"And you should return to the house. It is late and you are cold," Jason said, having followed in her footsteps.

"But I think I should stay a while longer. To be sure Dumpling has recovered," Georgina protested.

"Jackson, will the mare be all right?" Jason asked in preemptory tones.

"Aye, my lord, she'll do," came the gruff reply.

"You see, Georgie? Dumpling will be fine. You must return to the house."

"You sound like my father, Jason, and I can assure you—"

"ACHOO!"

Jason and Georgina whirled around to discover Nathaniel wiping his nose. "S-sorry," he said, sniffing. "I feel chilled."

"Oh, dear, are you ill, Nathaniel?" Georgina asked, hurrying over to him, her argument forgotten.

"No, of course not, I just—achoo!—just can't seem to get w-warm."

Georgina pulled her brother's coat closer about him and turned him toward the door. "We must get you back to the house. Mama used to warn me against the cold because of you. She said you always came down with a terrible cold every winter."

"Here now. That's not true. Just once or twice. And I don't need any cossetting either. I can—ACHOO!"

"Stop talking and walk quickly," Georgie said as she pushed him toward the door. Over her shoulder, she called, "Will you come help me, Jason? And Jackson, send word to the house if I am needed, please?" Before Jason could catch up with them, Georgina had shoved her brother from the stable out into the swirling snow.

Though it seemed they had spent hours in the stable, the household was still abroad when the wind swept the three of them inside. Georgina immediately ordered some broth from Cook and escorted her brother to his room, turning him over to his valet. "Someone will bring up the broth in a moment, Williams. Please put a hot brick in his bed and tuck him up at once," she ordered, ignoring the servant's affront that Miss Georgie would think he did not know what to do.

Jason, having assisted her in bringing Nathaniel to the house, stood waiting for her attention. When the valet closed the door, leaving the two of them in the hall alone, he grinned and said, "Don't you think you are acting too much the mother hen?"

With a considering look, Georgina explained, "Possibly, but only last winter a young lad on the estate took cold and died three days later. It is better to be safe than sorry."

"Perhaps you are right, but I feel Nathaniel will arise

in the morning, all trace of his cold having disappeared. After all, on the Continent we all suffered from the cold." He bit back the sudden memory that it had always taken Nathaniel longer than the others to recover.

"I hope you are in the right of it," Georgina said, giving him a doubtful look, "but it would not hurt you to take precautions also."

"Me?" Jason said, surprised. "I thought I was taking care of you."

Georgina laughed. "I appreciate the thought, Lord Chesterton," she said with a curtsy, "but I shall manage. I must go down and tell Papa about Dumpling's baby." She moved away from him before turning back. "Thank you for assisting me, Jason," she added, a sweet smile on her face.

"My pleasure, Georgina."

———

Georgina sat up in bed, a sense of well-being filling her. Dumpling's safe delivery and the tender newness of the tiny arrival polished the pleasure of the lazy warmth she felt as she snuggled down under the covers. Sharing her happiness with Nathaniel and Jason as well as her father increased her enjoyment.

Sometimes, particularly when her father buried his head in his studies, she had been lonesome. Now, for a while, she had Nathaniel and Jason. Even the fact that Jason still considered her a child could not dim her happiness this morning.

She shoved back the covers and swung her feet to the floor, grateful for the thick rug that covered it. Even with a fire burning merrily in the fireplace, her room felt as chilly as the frosted panes in her window.

Rubbing away the frost, she gazed with wonder on the first deep snow of the season. Her childhood memories of swooping down a hill on the sled Nathaniel had built and skating on the pond close to the house always made the first snow a magical time for her.

She jumped up and opened her wardrobe, anxious to start her day. She would begin with a visit to the stables to check on Dumpling and her foal. Dressed in boots, an old green wool gown almost too small for her curves and topped with her navy wool cloak, Georgina was soon outdoors. Jackson must have had his lads up early to have already cleared the path, she thought as she rushed into the comparative warmth of the stables.

Jason found her a few minutes later, kneeling in the hay, making friends with the shy filly. Dumpling stood nearby, an occasional nuzzle indicating her approval. Leaning over the half-door of the stall, he watched in silence until she looked up.

"Good morning. Wilkins said I would find you here."

Georgina stood. "Did you need me for something? Are you suffering from your exposure to the cold?"

"Of course not. I have never been in better health. I simply did not want to take my breakfast alone. Nathaniel and your father are not down yet."

"I will return to the house shortly. I only wanted to satisfy myself that Dumpling and her foal are well," Georgina explained.

"I am in no hurry." Jason watched the filly seek nourishment from its mother. "Have you named it yet?"

"No, I have been trying to think of a name for it. Jackson says it will shed the brown hair and look just like Dumpling. What do you suggest?"

"How about Blizzard? It describes the weather at its birth," Jason suggested with a smile.

"Blizzard? Hmmm, no, I don't think so," Georgina said, considering the word. "That sounds so—so cold.

And she is such a sweet filly." She reached out to stroke the filly as she spoke.

"You could give it a Christmas name. After all, Dumpling has given you a fine Christmas gift."

"Of course! What a wonderful idea, Jason. Now, what shall it be? Mistletoe? Yule?"

"I should not persist, but the French word for Christmas is Noel. Of course, since she is a filly, you would have to make it Noelle," he added, spelling out the word.

"Oh, Jason, that is perfect!" Georgina exclaimed, dancing over to hug him before running back to the newly named horse. "Noelle it shall be! How do you like your new name, my sweet," she crooned, ignoring the man standing as a statue at the door.

Jason was reminded of her response when he agreed to take on Albert. But instead of evoking the remembrance of a childish hug, he was discovering a more disturbing sweetness to her act. Her long auburn braid, left to hang down her back, caught his attention. The thought of how she would appear if her hair were loose about her shoulders invaded his mind, and he angrily rebuked himself for having such thoughts about a child.

"Well, now that we have named her, I am ready for breakfast. Shall we brave our snowy world, Jason?" Georgina asked gaily, pleased with life.

He silently offered her his arm. When she placed cold fingers there, he covered them with his own. "Where are your gloves, young lady?"

She smiled up at him, her brown eyes dancing. "I could not find them in my haste, so I came without them."

"I think you should knit yourself a pair of mittens, just as you are for the children. That would be most appropriate, since you are still a child yourself."

"If I am old enough to run my father's house and, I

might add, provide for your comfort, you cannot continue to call me a child," Georgina protested.

"You are a wonderful mistress of your father's house, Georgie, and well you know it, but I still see traces of the child I loved. You are not all grown yet."

She stared up into his eyes, a longing filling her. Would that love disappear when he realized she *was* grown? Shaking her head, she cast off such thoughts. "I have changed considerably from the scalawag I was that summer. Mama almost despaired of me."

Jason caught her chin between his fingers. "That scalawag stole my heart. I hope to never lose my memories of her."

Catching her breath at the sweetness of his words, Georgina was left speechless. They stood so, entranced in their own world, until Jackson entered the stable.

"Morning, my lord," the old man said. "We have a fine filly, don't we?"

"An excellent one, Jackson, thanks to your skilled hands. If you ever should want another position, you have only to come to me."

The stableman grunted in appreciation, but Georgina, having recovered her balance, took exception to her guest's words. "Well, I find it the height of ingratitude to sup at our table and try to steal our best people. The next thing I know you will try to entice Albert away from us."

"Not likely, my dear," Jason said dryly.

Georgina only giggled, having expected some such remark. With a goodbye to Jackson, the pair opened the stable door. A sparkling white world greet them.

"Isn't it gorgeous!" Georgina enthused. "Jason, do you skate?"

"I have been known to do so on occasion. Is there a suitable pond nearby?"

"Oh, yes, do you not remember the one just over that hill?" she asked, pointing westward. "I must ask Jackson to have someone check if it is safe for skating. I want to have a skating party."

"Aren't you a little old for such a thing?" he asked, a frown on his face.

"I thought you said I was still a child," Georgina reminded. He could not seem to make up his mind as to her age. A wicked idea popped into her head. They were approaching a line of fir trees that looked particularly fine against the white of the snow. She tugged her hand loose. "Excuse me one moment," she said urgently, and before Jason knew it, she had disappeared behind the nearest tree.

"Georgina, are you all right?" he demanded.

"Yes," she called. "I'll be right back—but don't look!"

Though he was concerned, Jason turned his back, as only a gentleman could when a lady requested he not look. He stared at the flower garden devoid of blooms and pulled his cape closer around him. It was cold. He hoped whatever was the matter would be quickly resolved. The lure of a warm fire and a hearty breakfast was growing stronger every moment.

Just as he was tempted to turn, only to see if she needed his assistance, he assured himself, a stinging plop of something wet hit his neck. Stunned, Jason reached up his hand to feel the remains of a perfectly formed snowball on the collar of his cape. And behind the fir tree, a look of wicked delight on her face, stood Georgina, primed to fire the next missile.

# Chapter Eight

"Georgina Denbigh, you wretch!" thundered the ever so sophisticated Lord Chesterton just before the soft plop of the second snowball broke against his chest. With no hesitation, he bent down to scoop a handful of snow and ran toward her hiding place, molding his weapon as he moved.

As he rounded the tree, he was met once more with a well-thrown ball of snow. By the time he recovered, his adversary was nowhere in sight. He moved forward quickly and was rewarded with a flash of navy blue cape behind the second tree. Though there was little target, he cast his snowball in frustration. As he leaned down to gather more snow, Georgina sailed another snowball over his head.

"Aha! You missed!" he crowed with all the glee of a schoolboy.

"Only because you bent over. I'll land the next one," she called back. Her strategy kept her moving toward the house with Jason in pursuit. She was wise enough to know if he ever got between her and her sanctuary, she was done for.

Jason, having studied under Wellington, the best of all strategists, had no difficulty understanding her plan. Therefore, he was determined to cut off her retreat. Stalking her movement, he held a snowball in each hand, waiting for sight of his quarry.

Georgina could not resist the target Jason suddenly presented. With speed, she hurled first one and then the other
snowball she had ready. But she underestimated her enemy.
Jason did not try to hide. He rushed his target, willing to
suffer her throws to gain the advantage.

Before Georgina knew what was happening, she found
herself prostrate in the cold snow, wrapped in Jason's arms.
No matter how she thrashed about, she could not free
herself from those steel bands.

"All right, young Georgie," he growled as she twisted
and turned, "you are about to receive your just desserts."
But the friction their two bodies created generated a
spreading warmth in Georgina, startling her. She grew
still, her brown eyes wide as she stared up into Justin's
face.

Jason recognized the warmth instantly and drew back
as if his prisoner had bitten him. Her soft lips trembled as
he stared down at her.

With an abrupt movement, he stood and pulled Georgina to her feet. "Go change out of your wet clothes," he
ordered sternly.

Georgina stared up at him. "I meant no harm, Jason."

"I know. And your aim has improved since you were
eight," he replied. "Now, be off with you before you are
sneezing like Nathaniel."

Georgina did not wait. Something strange had occurred
and she thought it best to follow Jason's instructions.

Jason remained standing among the fir trees, the cold
creeping inside his boots, waiting for the unexpected
warmth of desire to disappear. After all, Georgina Denbigh was a mere child. He could *not* have such thoughts
about her.

Her appearance of the evening before in a pale blue
muslin that displayed her womanly charms, her auburn

hair in curls, her glistening skin, contradicted him, and did nothing to dismiss his desire.

Damn! It must be because he was away from London, he concluded. As soon as Christmas was over, he would rush back to London before he did something stupid. After all, whatever her age, Georgina Denbigh was no lightskirt to satisfy his baser needs. And he had no desire to enter the state of marriage. That would be inviting even greater boredom than he had yet experienced.

————

When Georgina entered the breakfast room, she found her father and Jason enjoying their repast, but there was no sign of her brother. After greeting the other two, she asked, "Has Nathaniel already eaten?"

"I have not seen him," Mr. Denbigh answered, "and I arrived before Jason, so I assume he has not yet come down."

"I hope he has not caught a cold," Georgina murmured with a frown as she made her selections from the sidetable.

"If the two of you survived the cold last evening and again this morning, I am sure Nathaniel will do so as well."

"You must go see Dumpling's foal, Papa. Did Jason tell you its new name?"

"No, my dear, he didn't." Mr. Denbigh smiled at Jason. "I hope it is something more dignified than Dumpling."

"There is nothing wrong with Dumpling," Georgina defended her mare's name. "But we have named the baby Noelle for Christmas."

"An excellent choice," her father commended. "Thank you for guiding her, Jason."

Jason only smiled in reply. He had decided the less contact with Georgina the better.

Mr. Denbigh regarded him carefully, though Georgina seemed unaware of his unresponsiveness. "Papa, do you expect Anne and Tabitha to come over today since Mr. Twickenham is in residence and—and with everything that occurred yesterday?"

"I think so, my dear. Anne promised to try."

"How are Mrs. Hansen's drawings working out for you?" Jason asked, hoping such an innocuous subject would bore Georgina and send her on her way all the earlier. She was much too distracting in her plum wool gown with its high lace collar.

"Splendidly," Mr. Denbigh said with great enthusiasm. He continued to praise Mrs. Hansen's work and expound on the subject matter of his book for half an hour. Georgina finished her breakfast but sat at the table with the two men, enjoying listening to her father.

They were interrupted by Wilkins announcing the arrival of Tabitha and Mrs. Hansen. Mr. Denbigh rose at once to escort his co-worker to the library, leaving Tabitha to the other two.

"I'm glad you came, Tabby. Shall we go into the front parlor? I will have Wilkins bring a new pot of tea," Georgina offered.

"Thank you, Georgie," she replied, finally raising her eyes to look around the room.

Jason took pity on her shyness and gave her the information she sought. "Nathaniel has not yet come down to breakfast, Tabitha."

"Oh! I didn't . . . that is, thank you, Jason," she said as she met the kindness in his look.

"Perhaps you could check on him, Jason, while Tabitha has a cup of tea. Then the two of you could join us in the parlor,'' Georgina suggested, grateful for some time alone with her friend.

Jason, relegated to errand boy, gladly agreed, reminding himself he did not want to spend time alone with Miss Georgina Denbigh.

Georgina rushed Tabitha into the parlor. She assisted in removing her cloak and gasped in admiration. Her friend was clothed in a pale peach muslin gown, empire-style, with particularly fine French lace on the scooped neck, and small puffed sleeves. Its color enhanced Tabitha's silvery fairness and drew attention to her china blue eyes. To chase away the cold, she had wrapped a dark blue silk shawl around her shoulders.

''That is a new gown, Tabby, and it is beautiful!''

Tabitha's cheeks grew crimson. ''I had it made just recently—and—I thought—I wanted to look nice today,'' she finished lamely.

Georgina ignored the niceties. ''Are you unhappy about marrying Nathaniel?''

''Oh, no!'' Tabitha gasped. ''That is, I doubt I could withstand Papa if I did not want to, but—but I admire your brother greatly, Georgie. And we will be sisters.'' She bravely looked at her friend. ''Are you unhappy about it?''

''Of course not, you goose,'' Georgina said fondly. ''If it will make you happy, I am delighted. But I was concerned that you hoped for more than a marriage of convenience from Nathaniel and—''

Tabitha's even deeper blush caused Georgina to break off. She rushed to her side and clasped her hand. ''I am sorry, Tabby. I didn't mean to hurt you!''

Tabitha, having spent most of the night thinking about her situation and discussing it with Anne, placed her hand on Georgina's arm. ''Please, Georgie, there is no need to be concerned. I understand that your brother is making a marriage of convenience. Anne and I discussed it, and I have a plan.''

''A plan? Whatever do you mean?''

''Anne said that it was possible that I could teach your brother to care for me, if I strive to please him.''

''He should be striving to please you,'' Georgina said darkly.

''But, Georgie—''

''Good morning,'' Nathaniel said, interrupting their coze as he and Jason entered the parlor.

Tabitha rose and curtsied, her cheeks still red. ''Good morning, Nathaniel.''

''I trust you are—ACHOO!'' Nathaniel buried his face in his handkerchief. ''Excuse me,'' he finally offered.

While Georgina was concerned for her brother, it paled in comparison to Tabitha's alarm. ''Oh, my, Nathaniel, you have taken a cold,'' she exclaimed, rushing to his side. ''You should be in your bed. You must return to it at once.'' She placed her small hand on his arm to urge him toward the door.

''No, no, I refuse to be cossetted,'' he protested. ''I shall be all right.''

The timid Tabitha, armed with her concern, took charge. ''Well, I suppose it would be boring for you above stairs, but you must stay warm. Take the sofa by the fire. Georgie, would you have someone bring a coverlet for Nathaniel?''

Georgina agreed, though she expected her brother to protest. Instead, it appeared that Mr. Nathaniel Denbigh was enjoying his new fiancée's concern.

''Did you eat your breakfast?'' Tabitha demanded as she would to a recalcitrant child.

''No, I did not feel like breakfast.''

"Georgie, we will need a lot of tea, and perhaps Cook could send up some pastries, because Nathaniel must have nourishment."

"It is not as if we have tried to starve him, Tabby," Georgina protested. "He is always difficult when he doesn't feel well."

Tabitha seemed affronted that her friend would criticize Nathaniel. While she assisted him to the sofa and requested Jason to add wood to the fire, Georgina went in search of Wilkins.

―――――

Mr. Denbigh looked up from his work at his large desk and studied the woman sitting across the room from him. She had offered to read his latest writing to better understand the kind of drawing he needed, but instead she was staring at the wall across from her. It was not the first time that morning he had found her distracted.

"Anne, is there something wrong?"

She jumped in surprise. "Oh, no, Alistair. Your writing is quite clear. I—I was just thinking about my sketch."

He rose from his chair and crossed the room to sit beside her on the sofa. "Anne, my dear, I know I am a prosy old man, but I have had some experience with Georgina. If there is anything I can help you with, please be assured I am perfectly willing to do so."

A smile fluttered on Anne Hansen's pleasant face. It had been a long time since anyone had offered her support. "No, thank you. I shall manage."

"Was Mr. Twickenham disturbed that you came to us today?"

"No," Anne replied. "He believes we came to allow Tabitha to spend time with Nathaniel."

"He does not know you are working with me?"

Again she shook her head, saying nothing.

"Are you concerned that he will not allow you to continue doing so if he finds out?" Alistair Denbigh probed.

"It really does not matter, does it? After all, when Tabitha marries, my job will be at an end."

"Ah. You are concerned with your future," he concluded, a frown on his face.

With a rueful shrug of her slender shoulders, Anne smiled briefly at her companion. "I admit I am working out what I shall do."

"May I offer a suggestion?"

Anne Hansen could use assistance in her precarious situation, but she was reluctant to take charity from this man. "I shall manage, truly, Alistair. You have no need to be concerned."

"I'm sure you shall, my dear, but I, too, have been thinking about the future. And Nathaniel will want to discuss this with you."

"Nathaniel?"

"I believe he will want you to move here after the wedding and assist Tabitha for a while, instructing her in the art of managing the two estates. She will find you of great assistance, I'm sure."

Before Anne could protest, Mr. Denbigh raised his hand to stop her. "And, of course," he added with a twinkle in his eye, "that means we may continue our work with even greater convenience."

Anne responded with a laugh. His solution was admirable and she would enjoy it greatly had she truly believed she was needed. But she had instructed Tabitha in the art of housekeeping since her arrival almost a year ago. She knew her protegé would manage very well without her assistance. "Thank you, Alistair, but Tabitha is well versed in housekeeping. I think you will be surprised at her competence."

"There will be much to do with both estates at her bidding," he reminded her.

"Yes, but she will also have Georgie to assist her. And I believe Georgie could manage ten estates and still have time to attend all the social events in the county."

Mr. Denbigh considered the woman before him. Finally, he said, "I do not expect Georgie to remain with us all that long, you know. She is of marriageable age."

Anne stared at him, her eyebrows raised. "Yes, but she has never shown a preference for any of the men who have pursued her."

"No, she has not. Her brother is determined to take her to London in the spring, though now that he is to be married, I am not sure he will do so."

"Oh, dear. Tabby will hate returning to London. She has horrible memories of her time there."

"Yes, so Georgie has said. I believe it would be preferable to find Georgina a husband here rather than spend the spring in London."

Anne leaned back against the sofa, a frown on her face. "But I really do not feel any of the young men I have met are up to Georgina's weight." When she noticed Alistair's eyes on her, she blushed. "I apologize for my remark. I did not mean to offend."

"You haven't. You only said what I have often thought." He removed a piece of lint from his blue superfine jacket while saying, "I was thinking of someone a little closer to home."

Anne's eyes widened as she understood his meaning. "Do you think he is interested? I was not sure he is willing to consider marriage."

"Neither am I, my dear. But there is something there when he and Georgie are in the same room." He patted her hand. "Never mind. It is only a thought. But you can

see that you will be needed here. So do not concern yourself with your future. We have no intention of letting you
get away." With a warm smile, he rose from the sofa and
returned to his desk.

Anne stared after him. His words were comforting, but
they did not solve her problems. She had kept to herself
her admiration for Mr. Denbigh. Though he was ten years
her senior, she was comfortable with him, and even felt
the stirrings of passion when he was near. He was the
opposite of her late husband, an outdoorsman with no patience for books. While Mr. Denbigh was an active man,
managing his estate, riding to hounds and taking long
walks in his study of nature, he was intelligent and interested in more than horses.

With a sigh, Anne turned her eyes to the words on the
paper in her lap. Unfortunately, it was that attraction to
Mr. Denbigh that made it impossible to accept his plan.
Her pride would not allow his assistance when what she
wanted from him was so much more.

======

Georgina looked up from her knitting in disgust. More
than an hour had passed since Tabitha's arrival, and it had
all been spent tending to the invalid. She wanted her
brother to have a care of his health, but Tabitha was waiting on him every moment, even feeding him herself. And
much to Georgina's surprise, the normally difficult Nathaniel was lapping up her treatment.

"Do you think perhaps another pillow would make you
more comfortable, Nathaniel?" Tabitha asked.

"No, no, I am quite comfortable, Tabitha," he responded, "though—"

"What is it? I will see to whatever you need," the young
woman earnestly assured her fiancé, leaning forward from

her chair. She had no idea how attractive a picture she presented for his eyes.

"I wondered if you might read something to me. It would take my mind off my illness."

"Of course I will," Tabitha agreed. "What would you like me to read? Poetry?"

Georgina did not think she could bear her friend reading poems to her brother the rest of the morning, so she intervened with a suggestion of her own. "Why do you not read *Pride and Prejudice*? It is a new novel that I recently purchased in Sheffield, and I found it most amusing."

"A novel?" Jason asked, a smile on his face. "Does your father allow you to read those romantical writings?"

"Yes, he does," Georgina replied. "In fact, he read this book himself and pronounced it quite enjoyable."

"Then I hope you will choose to read this estimable book, Tabitha. I cannot wait to be so entertained."

Georgina refused to respond to his teasing and returned her attention to her knitting. But Nathaniel agreed with his friend, and Tabitha asked for her copy of the suggested book. Putting aside her knitting, Georgina chose to fetch it herself. She had sat in the stifling room much too long, listening to her brother play the invalid.

The rest of the morning passed pleasantly enough, enlivened by Miss Austen's writings. Georgina continued with her knitting and the two men relaxed as Tabitha read the story of the family with five daughters. In truth, Georgina thought it was best that her brother conserve his energy until he was over his cold, but she was astounded at his compliance. And Tabitha, in the past so shy when in the same room with men, seemed completely at her ease. Perhaps her brother's invalidism was the best thing all round.

At luncheon, Tabitha sat beside Nathaniel, urging him

to eat, ignoring the others. Georgina, at the foot of the table, opposite her father, was left to Jason for conversation. Her father and Anne were involved in discussion of their project.

"Do you suppose those two will be happy together after all?" Jason murmured.

Georgina glanced at her brother and friend. "I hope so. I am amazed at this morning's events."

"I am also somewhat surprised. Normally Nathaniel is most impatient with coddling."

"And Tabitha is generally so painfully shy."

"Perhaps she is unused to a suitor. Do you have suitors?" he abruptly asked.

Frowning, Georgina replied, "That is an improper question. Why do you ask?"

"I have seen no sign of them, and I wondered."

"I beg your pardon. Shall I invite several over so that you may believe that there is someone who considers me grown up?" Georgina's patience had been severely tested by the morning's events and she had none to spare for Jason.

"I was not attempting to insult you, Georgina," he said stiffly. "I was curious, that's all."

Miffed, Georgina turned her attention to her food and ignored her companion. The other two couples seemed unaware of the discontent at one end of the table, and the meal was soon completed.

The afternoon took on a different pattern. Tabitha insisted Nathaniel retire to his room for a nap, and he reluctantly agreed, leaving Georgina to wonder if his sickness was more serious than she had thought. She invited her friend to inspect Dumpling's new baby, and Jason retired to his room to supervise Albert's handling of his wardrobe—a precarious operation at best.

Anne and Tabitha left with the promise to return the next day. Tabitha considered it out of the question for Nathaniel to visit her, and Anne needed to come to Greenbriar Manor to work with Mr. Denbigh.

More of *Pride and Prejudice* was read the next morning as the four gathered in the parlor. In fact, everyone was quite happily settled when Wilkins interrupted them to announce Mr. Twickenham's arrival.

The news had an unhappy effect on Tabitha, causing her to retreat into the shy and timid young lady of earlier days. Nathaniel shoved the coverlet from his legs, not wanting to appear the invalid in front of his future father-in-law. Georgina put aside her knitting with a sigh. Only Jason seemed unaffected by their visitor.

Mr. Twickenham entered the room like a strong wind, disturbing everything. He greeted the two gentlemen who rose to bow to him and nodded to the ladies.

"I'm here to set the date for the wedding," he said bluntly.

"Oh, Papa," Tabitha said with a sigh, her cheeks crimson.

"Of course, Mr. Twickenham. I would have called on you before now, but—but I caught a cold and—"

Mr. Twickenham frowned at his future son-in-law. "You ain't sickly, are you? Don't want to have to find some other fellow to come up to scratch."

"No! No, of course I am not sickly," Nathaniel protested, anger erasing his discomfort.

"Good. Now, as I see it, I'll have my lawyers draw up our agreement and I can also pick up a special license at the same time. That way, when I come back, we can have the wedding, and then I'll not have to return to this godforsaken place again."

Even Jason was stunned by Mr. Twickenham's words.

"My dear sir, surely you would not marry your daughter off in such a—a havey-cavey manner."

"Don't believe in wasting time. You young fellows change your minds a lot."

"Sir," Nathaniel protested, enraged, "you have my word that I will marry your daughter."

"There's many a slip twixt the cup and the lip, young man. I'm a wise old codger in the ways of the world." Mr. Twickenham gave a satisfied nod and sat down.

Nathaniel stared at the man, wondering if he had taken leave of his senses. Georgina took pity on her brother and friend. "Mr. Twickenham, since the roads are so precarious in winter, why do you not remain in London until spring? My brother will have the bans called, and then when you return we will have the wedding. The spring is a lovely time for one."

"Spring be damned! Pardon, miss, for my rough tongue, but I'll have none of that. Besides, your brother's not going to want to be behindhand with the planting."

"But I could direct the operation of your land along with mine until the wedding, Mr. Twickenham," Nathaniel eagerly assured him.

"Nay, you'll not touch my land until it becomes yours."

Georgina, Nathaniel, and Jason looked at each other in exasperation while Tabitha hid her face in her hands. She knew from past experience how stubborn her father could be.

"Send for your father, young man. He'll make you see reason," Mr. Twickenham suggested.

Everyone approved of that idea, and Georgina rose to do Mr. Twickenham's bidding.

"Wait a minute!" the gentleman called as she was about to leave the room. "Where's Mrs. Hansen? Why isn't she here chaperoning my girl?"

No one was disposed to answer that question, but after a moment of silence, Georgina said, "We did not feel the need of a chaperone, Mr. Twickenham, especially since my brother and Tabitha are now affianced. Mrs. Hansen is—is looking at my father's work. He is preparing a book on plant life and Mrs. Hansen has a particular fondness for plants."

"And who is chaperoning *her*?" Mr. Twickenham demanded.

# Chapter Nine

Into the stunned silence, Georgina murmured, ''I'll fetch my father,'' and slipped from the room. She raced down the hall and opened the library door without knocking.

''Papa, Anne, Mr. Twickenham is here!''

Mr. Denbigh looked up from his desk where he was working, an abstracted look on his face. ''Yes, my dear?''

Anne, however, was more cognizant of the difficulties the man could bring into her life. She put aside her work and rose from the sofa. ''I'll come at once.''

The tension on Anne's face alerted Alistair Denbigh as his daughter's words had not. ''What is the matter, Anne?''

''You both must come. Papa, he is insisting Nathaniel and Tabitha be married by special license. And—and he is upset that Anne is here with you without a chaperone.''

''But that is ridiculous!'' Mr. Denbigh protested, his eyes taking in Anne's red cheeks and worried look. ''Anne is much too young and attractive—'' He broke off as both women looked at him and his own face flushed. ''We'll both come.''

Silence had reigned in the parlor after Georgina's departure. Mr. Twickenham paced up and down the Aubusson carpet, a ferocious frown on his face, occasionally muttering words under his breath. The three remaining watched him out of the corners of their eyes and waited for the arrival of the others. There was no attempt to reason with the man.

Mr. Denbigh escorted the two ladies into the large room and moved to Mr. Twickenham, his hand extended in greeting. However, Mr. Twickenham would have none of that. He stared first at the hand and then at the gentleman offering it.

"Sir, I'll not shake hands with the man who has offered me such a trick behind my back!"

Mr. Denbigh frowned. "I beg your pardon, Mr. Twickenham, but what is it that I have done?"

"As if you didn't know!" he returned in disgust. "I find you in private with my fiancée and you don't know what you've done! I'll tell you, sir—"

"Mr. Twickenham!" Mrs. Hansen interrupted, moving to stand in front of the distraught gentleman. "For the last time, I have not accepted your proposal."

"Aye, but you're a shy puss. I know how it is with you womenfolk. But don't you go letting this gentleman turn your head. Has he done anything he oughtn't?"

"Mr. Twickenham!" Anne exclaimed, outraged. "Mr. Denbigh has been all that is gentlemanly, and I'll not have you insult him in such a fashion. If you must know, I have been working for him, drawing the plants about which he is writing."

"But you're working for me!"

Anne turned to her second employer. "Mr. Denbigh, I am sorry. I would not have had you so insulted for anything."

"Never mind, my dear. But do you plan to marry Mr. Twickenham?" Alistair Denbigh was not even aware that he was holding his breath for her answer until she spoke.

"No! Never will I accept such an offer. And I have told him so repeatedly."

Mr. Twickenham ignored her. "A'course she'll marry me. I've a fine fortune to lay at her feet. She's just playing the coquette, you know. Besides," he added, a smug look on his face, "when my Tabitha marries, she'll have nowhere else to go."

Jason spoke up. "That is ungentlemanly of you, sir, to take advantage of her difficult circumstances and force her acceptance of your proposal."

"I ain't a gentleman. But I'm a fair and square dealer. She'll have everything her heart desires once she becomes my bride." He turned back to Mr. Denbigh. "I'll take Mrs. Hansen's word that nothing unseemly went on here. So, we'll just get down to business on my original purpose for this call, shall we?"

Stunned by the man's words, not even Mr. Denbigh had a reply. Anne Hansen moved as far away from him as possible, turning her back as she stared out the window. Georgina joined Tabitha on the sofa, taking her hand in comfort.

Mr. Twickenham filled the awkward silence. "I was telling your son that I can return with a special license in a few days time and we can tie the little agreement up right and tight."

Mr. Denbigh, instead of responding, turned to Mrs. Hansen. "Anne, would you take Georgina and Tabitha upstairs, please? I believe the discussion will progress better without their presence."

All three women silently blessed Mr. Denbigh as they hurried to do his bidding. Once the door closed behind them, he turned to Mr. Twickenham.

"Sir, may we know the reason for such unseemly rush?"

"Certainly, you may. I've already explained it to that young jackanapes, but he don't seem to understand. I've only visited here a'cause of my daughter, or more rightly, Mrs. Hansen. I don't like the country. No need to draw out this affair. Besides, that way I'm sure your boy won't back out of our little agreement."

When Nathaniel would have once again protested this slur upon his honor, his father waved him away. "I see. And you have no concern about how such a rushed marriage will appear to our neighbors?"

"No concern of mine. I don't intend to ever see them again. They didn't take to the likes of me, anyhow."

"But your daughter, sir?" Mr. Denbigh reminded him, finding it difficult to believe the man could be so callous.

"She'll have no complaints. Never expected her to make any kind of marriage at all after that disaster in London."

Mr. Denbigh looked at his son and saw there outrage at the man's words. He, too, was appalled, but he decided it would be better to go along with the man's plan. The sooner they were rid of Mr. Twickenham, the better it would be for all concerned.

"All right, sir, when you return with the agreement and the special license, my son and your daughter will be married."

"Papa!"

"Mr. Denbigh, you cannot have thought—"

"Good. In addition to the land, I'll include twenty thousand pounds in Tabitha's dowry. Nobody will ever say Horace Twickenham is a cheapskate!" The man beamed at all three men in the room before extending his hand to Mr. Denbigh. "I know you'll forgive my refusing to shake your hand earlier."

Mr. Denbigh shook hands but felt the veriest schemer

when he knew he would offer his assistance to Mrs. Hansen to avoid marriage with this man at all cost.

"Well, then, I'll just be on my way. Tell Tabitha I'm leaving for London and I'll return as soon as possible. After all, I know she's anxious for her wedding day." Before anyone could respond, the man strode from the room.

"Papa! How could you have agreed to such a thing?" Nathaniel demanded as soon as the man was gone.

"How much choice did we have? Would you renounce Tabitha now? Are you willing to give up the Buxton estate?"

"No, of course not, but we should have refused to agree to such a thing."

"Then you would have lost everything," Mr. Denbigh said with a sigh. "Mr. Twickenham is a stubborn man, and I could not face Tabitha now and tell her we were withdrawing our offer."

Nathaniel's face paled at the thought. "No, of course not. It is unthinkable, but I don't know if the neighbors will ever accept her with such a hasty marriage."

"Of course they will. We will work out a plan. Ring for Wilkins and have him request the ladies to join us. And ask for a tea tray." He paused until Nathaniel moved away.

Mr. Denbigh looked at Jason. "What think you, Jason? Can we pull it off?"

"If we were in London, it would be more difficult, but I believe it is possible here. After all, you and your family have a reputation in good standing with the community, and I cannot believe Tabitha has been taken in dislike. When she accompanied Nathaniel and myself as we rode round the estate, she was well received."

"True. Bless the child, she has worked with Georgie

helping our families and hers almost since she first arrived. She is a good-hearted girl.''

"Then I feel sure the neighbors will treat her kindly. But it is important that it is announced at once. Would it be possible to have some kind of entertainment where that could be done?''

Before Mr. Denbigh could answer, Nathaniel turned back from their discussion with Wilkins. Mr. Denbigh explained their beliefs to him.

With a sigh, Nathaniel concurred. "I suppose you are right. That is one of the reasons I willingly agreed to marry Tabitha. She seems to care about the people and they received her very well. But how will we explain the hasty marriage?''

Jason grinned. "Why not sacrifice Mr. Twickenham? Tell them the truth. He is demanding a quick marriage so he will not be bothered anymore with the country estate or his daughter. And it might make everything more readily acceptable if you and Tabitha were more—more romantic with each other.''

"You mean pretend to be in love?'' Nathaniel asked, horrified.

"I believe Jason has a point, son,'' Mr. Denbigh said. "The ladies in particular will forgive anything if it is for love.''

Since three very anxious ladies entered the room at that moment, the conversation was halted.

Though Tabitha and Anne stared in mute appeal, it was Georgina who demanded information.

"What has happened, Papa?''

Mr. Denbigh offered all three chairs before saying calmly, "We have agreed to Mr. Twickenham's request.''

"What?'' Georgina almost screamed while Tabitha gasped.

"Tabitha, I hope you will forgive my plain speaking. Your father is a stubborn man. Had we not agreed, it is possible he would have refused to allow you to marry Nathaniel."

Mr. Denbigh demanded smelling salts when Tabitha's face grew pale. Anne Hansen dug in her reticule and waved hers beneath Tabitha's nose.

As her color returned, Mr. Denbigh continued. "I believe we shall be able to satisfy our neighbors as to the necessity for speed if we tell them it is your father's fault. Will that offend you, my dear?" he asked Tabitha gently.

"No—no, I think that is the appropriate thing to do," Tabitha said with surprising strength.

"Good. Now, Georgina, we need some kind of entertainment at once, where we can announce the marriage. Can you plan a dinner party?"

"Yes," she replied, "but—Papa, how about a skating party? I meant to ask you about it earlier. The pond is frozen and we can serve supper here after the skating."

"That is more informal than I intended, but it might do very well. What do you think?" he asked the others.

Everyone seemed in agreement, so Mr. Denbigh began to marshal his forces. "Good. Write out the invitations at once, Georgie. Or perhaps you could enlist Anne and Tabitha in that task so you may prepare the menu with Cook. Jason and Nathaniel shall oversee the preparation of the pond and a gathering of wood for several bonfires. We'll need hot drinks served to help keep everyone warm. And some benches for non-skaters to sit on."

As everyone rose to attend to his or her duties, Mr. Denbigh added, "There is just one more thing."

There was a general shuffling as everyone subsided back into his chair.

"Jason has made a very good point. Our neighbors are

predisposed to take our side in any controversy, but it might make them even more so if—'' he paused to carefully observe his future daughter-in-law, ''—Nathaniel and Tabitha were to appear to be in love with each other. And the rest of us can support that by letting our closest acquaintances know that it is a love match.''

Tabitha's eyes grew huge and her cheeks crimson. When Nathaniel looked at her, she swiftly dropped her lashes to cover her thoughts. Anne Hansen saw the look of appeal Mr. Denbigh cast her. ''I agree, Alistair. That is quite the best plan. When you combine their love with Mr. Twickenham's stubbornness, I feel sure everyone will think they are doing the right thing.''

''Good! Then we must all be about our duties.''

There was a general rush to the door, several people avoiding everyone else's eyes.

''Let's go to the morning room,'' Georgina suggested to the other two women. ''My writing things are there, and we'll make a list of guests.''

Tabitha scurried after the other two, but she was not fast enough to avoid Nathaniel, who caught her by the arm. ''Tabitha?''

''Yes, Nathaniel?'' she answered in a low voice, her eyes shuttered.

''You do still want to marry me, don't you?''

The anxiety in his voice gave her courage and she looked up into his face. ''Yes, Nathaniel, I do. I know I should not say it, but I will be so glad to never have to obey my father again. And—and I will love living here.'' That was the closest she could come to expressing her feelings about the man beside her.

''I am glad. And you will not find it too difficult to pretend being in love?''

With a smothered giggle, brought on by rising hysteria,

Tabitha replied, "No, Nathaniel, that will be easy enough." She snatched her arm from his grasp and fled down the hall, afraid she had given herself away.

Jason surveyed the scene before him. Brightly garbed skaters covered the ice of the Denbigh's large pond, moving in graceful circles. Their breaths rose in frosted smoke as much chatter and laughter was heard. Only a short distance from him was a roaring fire, constantly fed by servants. Maids dispensed hot apple cider and tea, along with Cook's pastries.

His eyes narrowed as Georgina Denbigh floated by on the arms of one of her admirers. There was no longer any need to ask if the young lady had suitors. Jason, who had intended to skate with her, found he would have to wait his turn.

Mr. Nathaniel Denbigh, on the other hand, never left the side of his partner, Tabitha Twickenham. Their devotion to each other had been much remarked by their neighbors. Both Mr. Denbigh and Mrs. Hansen had told a few acquaintances of the engagement, even though it would not be announced until the party moved indoors.

Jason checked his skates. It was time he make his presence felt by a certain young lady, he decided. He had convinced himself that his earlier panic was nonsensical, caused by a longing for his mistress rather than anything to do with Georgie. Stepping to the edge of the pond, he moved out on the ice, cutting across the parade of skaters and gliding up behind Georgina and her latest swain.

"I believe it is time to share your partner, sir," he said with a smile at the young man struggling to keep up with Georgina's fluid motion.

"Oh, of course, my lord," the young man said, releasing her arm at once. He stood in awe of such a splendid Corinthian as Lord Chesterton.

With a gracious nod, Jason took her arm and glided across the ice, leaving the suitor far behind. "How did you manage to skate with him without falling?" he asked.

"Robert may not be an excellent skater, my lord, but he is kind," Georgina responded, her eyes straight ahead.

"Oh-ho, are you on your ropes, Georgie? What have I done to displease you?"

"Nothing at all. I just do not want you to sneer at Robert. He is a very nice man."

"I promise not to do so. How do you think our plan is working?" Jason asked, glancing at those around him.

"Very well. Several people have commented on Nathaniel's devotion to Tabby. She is very well-liked despite Mr. Twickenham."

"I believe your father has mentioned their engagement to several people."

"Yes, and Anne has been explaining the circumstances to a few of the ladies. I believe by the time we announce the engagement, everyone will join us in wishing them happy."

"And villifying Mr. Twickenham?" Jason asked with a laugh.

"If they do, it is his fault," Georgina said firmly, just before a young man fell on the ice right in front of her. Jason pulled her tightly against him and skated around the unfortunate fellow. Georgina gave him a breathless thank you.

"My pleasure, Georgie. It is much warmer when you skate closer to me."

"We have provided a fire to warm you, Jason," she replied sweetly.

"We? I supervised the gathering of firewood and the

building of the fire, my dear, not you. You had the nice, warm chore of planning the menu."

Laughing up into his face, Georgina said, "You needed the exercise, I'm sure."

"Oh, really?" Jason sped up his skating, perforce moving Georgina at a fast pace also. "We shall see who needs the exercise, young lady."

"Jason," Georgina gasped, "you are going too fast!"

Jason guided his partner away from the crowd and skated all the faster, enjoying the wind blowing in their faces in spite off its sharp edge. "Do you admit that I have no need of exercise?"

"Yes! Yes, you are in fine fettle, even if you arc spoiled!" she agreed, laughing. "Please slow down."

By this time they had reached the far end of the pond where it narrowed and turned. Surrounded by trees, this area was cut off from the view of everyone at the other end. Jason swung his partner around the curve and then came to an abrupt halt. There beneath the trees were Nathaniel and Tabitha, kissing.

Disturbed by the sudden motion, the two sprang apart and then fell onto the ice. Jason and Georgina rushed over to help them to their feet.

"Sorry, old boy. I didn't mean to interrupt your courting," Jason assured his friend under his breath.

"Just what did you intend doing away from everyone else?" Nathaniel asked, irritated.

Jason's cheeks turned almost as red as Nathaniel's. "Nothing! I—that is, I was teasing Georgie, that's all."

Nathaniel cast him a look that scorned his answer and turned his attention to Tabitha. "Are you all right, Tabby?"

"Yes, Nathaniel. I am fine. Did you hurt yourself?"

"No. Let's go warm by the fire. We should be returning to the house soon."

Ignoring the other two, the affianced couple skated back to the fire.

"Well, shall we join them, Georgie?" Jason asked, holding out his arm.

"I suppose so," she said, her mind on the scene they had just interrupted.

"Is anything the matter?"

"Why do you suppose Nathaniel was kissing Tabby?" she abruptly asked.

Jason smothered the laughter that immediately rose in his throat. "They are to be married, Georgie. Married people do kiss, you know."

"I know that. But do you think he was kissing her to pretend, as we planned, or because he has come to love her?"

Jason looked down at his companion, her eyes raised questioningly to his, her cheeks ruby red from the cold, framed in a scarlet cloak, its hood trimmed in ermine, and he came to a stop. "Sometimes, Georgie, a man is simply tempted by the beauty of the young lady." He paused but she did not move. "Like now," he added softly, his lips descending to hers.

Georgina held her breath, her eyes fixed on his. At the last minute, Jason jerked his head away and muttered, "Forgive me!"

Her eyes widening in pain at the sudden rejection, Georgina pulled away from her partner and hurried toward the fire.

Jason caught up with her easily and took her arm in spite of her protests. "If we do not return together, it will be remarked upon. And you do not need more gossip about your family at the present time."

"Very well," she agreed, but stared straight ahead.

She broke away from him without a word when the bonfire was reached. With relief, she heard her father calling everyone to dinner. There was a large wagon covered with hay waiting to take the skaters back to the manor house that glowed in the dusk, candles in its windows.

Georgina joined a crowd of young people, several young men begging her to sit next to them. Lord Chesterton made no attempt to join her. He found her too tempting for his peace of mind.

Well-laid fires burned in the hearths and a bountiful feast was waiting in the dining hall. Their guests wandered through the several parlors and morning room opened for their comfort. Georgina kept a watchful eye on the buffet, quick to have every dish refilled. Her father presided over the huge silver wassail bowl in which he had blended his special Christmas punch. When everyone was served, he tapped on a crystal glass with a spoon to gain their attention.

"My friends," he began, a bright smile on his face, "not only have we asked you here to celebrate the coming holidays with us, but also to share in our happiness. My eldest, my son, has chosen his bride. May I offer a toast to Nathaniel Denbigh and the future Mrs. Denbigh, Miss Tabitha Twickenham!"

Well-primed with judicious gossip spread by Anne Hansen and Mr. Denbigh himself, there was an uproar of cheers. "Here, here!" they shouted, their cups raised high before a toast was drunk to the happy couple.

Georgina, standing to one side, was pleased to see how happy they both looked. Either they were superb actors, or they both were truly pleased about their coming union. Georgina wasn't sure she would have been so accepting. She wanted to know that the man she married loved her.

Marriages of convenience were common, but her father had loved her mother, and she wanted no less. Unfortunately, she had so far found no one she considered a possible mate. Her eyes swept over their guests, then halted when they met those of Jason. She turned her head away.

Jostled by someone advancing to congratulate the engaged couple, Georgina snapped out of her reflections. She circulated among their guests, answering questions and joining in the celebration. There would be time for her own problems later.

"Everything is going very well, thanks to your excellent planning, my dear," Mr. Denbigh whispered in her ear.

"I could not have done it all without Anne and Tabitha helping, Papa. But I believe everyone will accept their hurried marriage and place all the blame on Mr. Twickenham, where it belongs," Georgina said with a satisfied nod.

"I believe you are right, may God forgive us," he replied with a chuckle.

Their confab was interrupted by the arrival of several coachmen with the word that the snow had begun coming down heavily again. Hurried goodbyes were expressed, and the party ended rather abruptly.

When the last of their guests had departed, the Denbighs, Jason, Mrs. Hansen, and Tabitha returned to the parlor.

"I am glad we had planned on staying the night," Anne said. "I would not look forward to a carriage ride in the snow storm."

"Do you think it will snow much more?" Georgina asked her father.

"I do not know, my dear, but I would not object to a snow storm that would postpone Mr. Twickenham's arrival by a few days. It would give us time to catch our breaths."

There was general agreement to that statement.

# Chapter Ten

Mr. Denbigh got his wish. The area was visited with a ferocious snow storm that deposited two feet of snow, stopping all travel for almost a week.

Though Anne and Tabitha had come prepared for an overnight stay, they remained at Greenbriar Manor for several days and used a makeshift wardrobe from Georgina's gowns and the attic.

The third day, when Mr. Denbigh and Mrs. Hansen were hard at work in the library, he discovered her staring into the distance again. "Is anything worrying you, Anne?"

Startled, Anne blinked and then said, "No, of course not, Alistair. I was just thinking."

"Ah. Then you are not concerned about the upcoming marriage?"

"No, I think Nathaniel will make Tabitha happy. You see, he values her as her father never did. And while that might not be enough to satisfy some women, I think it will Tabby. And perhaps love will grow."

"You are a wise woman, my dear. I hope you are right. I will admit to some concern myself, but the longer I am in Tabitha's company, the more I have come to believe she will be a wonderful wife to Nathaniel . . . as long as her father remains in London."

Anne chuckled. "Yes, he does rather muddy the water, doesn't he?"

"Quite so."

"Do you think the roads will be passable tomorrow?" Anne asked abruptly, staring down at her hands.

"I don't think so. It is still snowing today, though lightly. Are you in such a hurry to leave us?"

"Oh, no! It is just that—that I was expecting a letter. I thought the post might arrive tomorrow."

"Is someone in your family ill?" Mr. Denbigh asked in concern.

"No."

Mr. Denbigh stared at his companion, but she neither raised her eyes to meet his nor said anything else. Without prying, he could not ask why the letter was so important to her.

Abruptly, she said, "I sent a letter to the firm that brought me here, asking their assistance in finding another position."

"But, Anne, I told you that we needed you. Are you not happy here?"

With a wavery smile, she replied, "Oh, Alistair, it is not that. You know I am very happy working here with you. But I must support myself, and I will soon be finished with the drawings you requested."

"And you do not feel you could remain and guide Tabitha through her first year as lady of the manor?"

"We have already discussed that. Georgina knows more about that than I do. And even if she marries, she will be here until late spring." She bowed her head, avoiding his eyes. "It will be best if I find somewhere else to work."

"I see. And you are not tempted by Mr. Twickenham's

wealth?'' Mr. Denbigh asked gently. ''It would save you from the drudgery of work.''

''Work is not the difficulty,'' Anne whispered. ''It is not belonging, not being part of a family. I am a hard worker, but—'' She broke off, closing her eyes to hold back the tears that formed there.

Mr. Denbigh lowered his pen to the desk and leaned back in his chair, hoping to stem the desire to rush to her side and take her in his arms. He was too old for such nonsense, he assured himself. With a nervous chuckle, he said, ''If I were not too old for you, I would offer you my family . . . and myself.''

Surreptitiously wiping away the few tears that had escaped, Anne said, ''And if you were not joking, I would accept.''

There was silence in the room, the words just spoken dashing to and fro as both examined them. Finally, Anne said, taking up her piece of charcoal again along with her pad, ''I am sorry to bother you with my problems when you have enough to deal with, Alistair. Please forgive my silliness.''

When there was no response, Anne dared to peep from under her lashes at the man who gave joy to her days. She discovered he was staring at her as if he could see through her. ''Alistair?''

''Did you mean it, Anne?'' he asked in a low voice.

''I beg your pardon?''

''I know I am too old for you, my dear, but would you prefer marriage to an old man and his family to finding a new position? Because if you would, I would delight in having you as my wife.''

Anne sat very still, as if any movement would break the spell. With her heart in her eyes, she whispered, ''Alistair, to remain with you forever would give me greater joy than anything on earth. I swear to you I would do my best to make you happy. I know your first marriage was—'' She never finished that sentence, because Mr. Denbigh had leaped from his chair like a man of twenty and joined her on the sofa.

After some time, Mr. Denbigh leaned back, his arm around Mrs. Hansen, her head on his shoulder. ''Oh, my dear, to think I almost didn't speak. I was afraid you thought me too old, too decrepit. I am fifty, you know,'' he said, as if confessing a shameful secret.

''And so you should be with a son as old as Nathaniel. In fact, I thought you might be older.''

''Older? And you still accepted me?''

Anne reached up to kiss his cheek. ''Whatever your age, you are perfect for me, my love. I have admired you for some time, but working with you has taught me the true meaning of love.''

Mr. Denbigh rewarded her words with another kiss. ''Elizabeth, my wife—my first wife,'' he added with a laugh, ''was a fine woman, and I loved her very much. But she would not begrudge me another love. Perhaps I will not make the mistakes of youth with you, my dear Anne.''

There was much more talk of their pasts and their future and the emotion that overflowed their hearts. It was not until Wilkins knocked on the door to announce luncheon that the outside world intruded upon their happiness.

''Oh, dear,'' Anne exclaimed, drawing back from Alistair's arms. ''When do we tell the others?''

''Why not now?''

''But—but shouldn't you tell Georgie and Nathaniel in private? I do not know how they will react.'' Anne chewed on her bottom lip as she considered their possible responses.

"They will be delighted, my dear. And we could not exclude Tabitha. She not only has been your concern for almost a year, but she also is to become a member of this family."

"I had forgotten!" Anne exclaimed in joy. "I will not be separated from Tabby! Oh, Alistair, is life not wonderful?"

Mr. Denbigh laughed. "At this moment, my love, I could not agree more. Though there have been times of loneliness in the past when I thought life had little meaning."

"I know." She sighed, leaning against him once more, enjoying the solid warmth of him.

"Come. If we do not join the others at once, I shall forget I am a gentleman and an old man and behave reprehensibly."

"And if you continue to label yourself old, I shall have to prove to you how young you are to me," Anne whispered, her arms around his neck, "and we will never arrive at the luncheon table."

Laughing joyously, Mr. Denbigh hugged his fiancée closely to him before pulling her up from the sofa. "I grow younger every minute. Let's go share our happy news with the others."

———

The four young people had put aside *Pride and Prejudice* for luncheon. Gathered in the dining room, they stood waiting for Mr. Denbigh and Mrs. Hansen to join them.

"Do you suppose Wilkins forgot to call them?" Nathaniel asked.

Georgina smiled at such a ridiculous thought but Tabitha replied, "I'm sure he did not forget. Perhaps they had to finish something before coming to luncheon."

Wilkins entered the room from the butler's pantry at that moment and then backed out again when he realized his master was not present. Before anything could be said, however, the door opened and the missing couple entered the room.

"Ah, we're late, aren't we? Sorry to keep you waiting, but something . . . delayed us," Mr. Denbigh said with a large smile. Anne avoided his eyes while she fought to hold back the blush she could feel in her cheeks.

Georgina eyed the couple with speculation. Somehow she felt sure their time in the library had not all been spent working. She turned to Tabitha and found a questioning look on her face.

"Are you all right, Anne?" Tabitha asked quietly.

"Oh, yes, I'm fine, Tabby dear," she said, though she didn't meet her charge's eyes. Mr. Denbigh held out her chair for her before Wilkins could do so, having reentered when he heard the additional voices.

Everyone's eyes were on their host, but Mr. Denbigh continued on as if everything were normal. The first course, a hearty potato soup, was served.

"Papa, how is your book progressing?" Georgina asked, her eyes on Anne rather than her father.

"Quite well, my dear. Thank you for asking. It is certainly convenient having Anne here to work with me."

"Yes, it is, isn't it? I don't know how we'll manage when she leaves."

Mr. Denbigh gazed at his youngest child with a twinkle in his eye. "I didn't think you intended her to leave, Georgie."

Georgina blinked twice before saying carefully, "What do you mean, Papa?"

"I thought it a ridiculous idea at the time, of course, since I am so much older than Anne, but I had the distinct impression that you and quite possibly Tabitha were matchmaking when you wanted me to see Anne's drawings."

Nathaniel stared first at his sister and then his intended, a frown on his face. "Surely you jest, Papa. Georgie would not attempt such a thing."

"Ah, then you agree that I am too old?" Mr. Denbigh asked calmly.

Nathaniel was at a loss for words, but his friend came to his rescue. Jason had been watching his fellow diners quite intently. He now said, "I'm sure Nathaniel meant that you and Mrs. Hansen are of an age and intelligence that such machinations are unnecessary."

"Diplomacy has lost an impressive talent in you, Jason. I hope some of your ability has rubbed off on Nathaniel, though I have yet to see it." Mr. Denbigh turned back to his daughter. "Well, Georgina, was I correct?"

"Yes, Papa, you were. Tabitha loves Anne and I love you. We wanted both of you to be happy, and—and it seemed to us that you were ideally suited. If we have caused you any embarrassment, I apologize, but truly, it was only because we love you both."

"Thank you, my child. You have never embarrassed me. And," Mr. Denbigh said, rising from his chair and moving to take Anne's hand, "you are correct. We feel we are ideally suited also. I am pleased to tell you that Anne has accepted my proposal."

There was joyous congratulations from the two young women, but the gentlemen were stunned by the news.

"But when will you marry?" Georgina asked as soon as they had all resumed their seats.

"We have not discussed that, though I see no reason to wait," Mr. Denbigh said.

"But we don't want to intrude upon your wedding," Anne assured Tabitha.

"Nonsense," Tabitha said, surprising everyone by her firmness. "I think we should make it a double wedding."

"Tabby, you wouldn't mind?" Georgina asked.

"Of course not. Nothing could give me greater pleasure than to see Anne happily settled on the same day as me."

"Nathaniel?" Mr. Denbigh asked.

"I will agree to whatever Tabitha wishes, Papa," Nathaniel said stiffly. "But, of course, you will have to secure a special license. You could ask Mr. Twickenham to bring two of them." Georgina frowned at the acidity in her brother's words.

"No, I don't think that would be appropriate, considering the circumstances," Mr. Denbigh said with a laugh. "I shall write my man of business in London and have him send it by messenger as soon as the roads clear. If Mr. Twickenham arrives beforehand, we will just explain that we must postpone the wedding for a few days."

"I don't think I want to assist you in that explanation," Jason murmured.

"Good God, no!" Nathaniel exclaimed, suppressing a shudder at the thought.

"Perhaps it would be best to tell him we have to wait for members of the family to arrive for the wedding," Anne suggested. "He might even decide to return to London rather than wait for the wedding to take place."

"Not a bad idea, my love," Mr. Denbigh said consideringly. "But I'll not allow him to hound you. We'll see how he reacts to the delay."

━━━━━

Georgina moved silently down the hall, looking both ways before rapping lightly on the closed door.

"Who is it?" her brother's voice called out.

"It's me, Georgina," she answered, leaning close to the door.

Nathaniel swung open the door. "Well?"

"I want to talk to you, Nathaniel. May I come in?"

"I suppose so, but I'm supposed to be resting," he grumbled as he moved back to allow her entry.

"So get back to bed. We can talk while you rest." Georgina followed him over to the bed and drew up a chair beside it. Nathaniel leaned on one elbow and frowned at his sister.

"If you are here to complain about—"

"What? Complain?" Georgina asked with mock innocence. "Whatever makes you think that?"

"You're always complaining about whatever I do," he muttered.

"How can you say that when I haven't seen you more than ten days in the past seven years?" Georgina demanded righteously.

"What do you want?" Nathaniel demanded, giving up a fruitless argument.

"I wanted to talk to you about Papa's marriage. You didn't seem pleased at luncheon."

"Must I become delirious with joy about every little thing?" He threw himself flat on the bed and stared at the ceiling.

"But Nathaniel—"

"What about Mama? She's only been dead a little while

and already Papa is marrying someone else. And the woman is almost half his age!"

"She is not. Anne is forty, and a lot of people marry with that age difference." Georgina paused to breathe deeply before she addressed the most serious of her brother's objections. "And you know I loved Mama as much as you, but Papa has been alone for four years. You have been away—"

"Well, I am back now! He does not need to marry to have companionship," Nathaniel snapped. Much to his surprise, his sister broke into laughter.

"Nathaniel?" Jason asked from the door, having swung it open. "Oh, sorry. I didn't know you had company," he said, backing out.

"No, Jason, come in. I think Georgina has gone crazy and you will have to protect me from her."

"Oh, really, Nathaniel," Georgina protested. "It is only that I did not agree with him, Jason."

Jason wandered over to the bed and gazed down at the lovely young woman smiling up at him. "Is he disturbed that you have conspired to trap your father into marriage?"

"That is another point!" Nathaniel exclaimed. "We left London because of such behavior. I never thought my sister would be guilty of it."

"Nonsense!" Georgina retorted. "Papa and Anne are very happy!"

"I did not think your father unhappy prior to his engagement," Jason commented in a superior manner, his eyes boring into Georgina.

"He was lonely. How can you not be happy for him? Didn't you see the joy on his face?" Georgina demanded, standing to stare at the two men.

"A woman always thinks a man is happy because he

has done what she wants. Marriage is a trap women have devised to bend men to their wills.''

Georgina stared at Jason, stunned by his words. When her brother nodded in agreement, she turned to leave the room. At the door, she paused to warn, ''Do not interfere with my father's happiness!'' Neither man spoke as she departed.

Frustrated and angered by her brother and his friend, Georgina donned her outdoors clothes and called Chester to heel. They both needed fresh air.

———

In a different part of the house, there was another discussion about the second upcoming marriage.

''Alistair, I don't think Nathaniel was happy about our announcement.''

Mr. Denbigh swung around from the bookshelf where he was replacing a rather hefty volume. ''Really?''

''Didn't you notice?'' Anne asked, willing to be convinced she was wrong.

''Yes, my dear,'' Alistair said with a smile, ''but I was hoping you had not.''

''Oh, dear. I—I suppose we should give up the idea, then,'' she replied bravely.

''Give up? Give up marrying?'' Mr. Denbigh asked before answering his own question. ''Not for a minute, my love.''

''But Alistair—''

''The only way I will give up marrying you, Anne, my dear, is for you to look me in the eye and tell me honestly and truly that you do not want to marry me.''

Rather than follow his directive, Anne turned away. ''But I do not want any of your family to be unhappy, Alistair.''

''Nor do I, but if they choose to be, there is nothing I

can do about it. I see no reason to be miserable myself."
Anne felt his warm hands on her shoulders as she was
turned around to face her fiancé. "And I would be ever
so miserable if I did not marry you, my love," Alistair
Denbigh promised as he kissed her gently.

Such a pronouncement had the fortuitous effect of causing Anne Hansen to forget any objections she felt compelled to make, and the next few minutes were delightfully
spent assuring each other of their love.

"We have not made much progress in our work," Mr.
Denbigh said ruefully as he sat beside his beloved on the
sofa a few minutes later.

"I will try not to distract you," Anne said earnestly,
moving to rise and return to her task.

Mr. Denbigh laughed as he pulled her back against him.
"I was not cracking the whip, my devoted slave."

"I know, but it is my fault."

"Anne," Mr. Denbigh protested, "you must relax
and ignore my words. I was only commenting, not complaining. This day has been the most delightful in a long
while. I can work any day. But heretofore, I have not
had the delight of, um, passing the time with you in my
arms."

She blushed delightfully, bringing a broad smile to her
companion's face. "I hope both my children are half as
lucky as me. I have found the joy of love twice in my life.
I am a most fortunate man."

"Do you think Mr. Twickenham will be difficult when
he returns?"

Mr. Denbigh sighed. "Well, I do not believe he will be
pleased with your news. He could not believe you would
refuse his offer. And he will not consider me the better
choice."

"Perhaps we should postpone our marriage until after he leaves? I do not want to ruin Tabitha's day."

"That would be a coward's choice, my love." He paused before saying, "But not a bad one, I must say. I think we may try postponing the wedding, and if he remains, keep our secret until the last moment."

Anne rested her head against the strong shoulders of her fiancé. "Whatever you think, Alistair."

"Spoken like a true wife, my love," he approved with a grin.

# Chapter Eleven

Georgina slipped out into a fairyland world where everything was covered with a blanket of whiteness. Snowflakes were now drifting lazily to join their cousins already on the ground, rather than the spitting fury they had been for the past several days. She drew a deep breath of the crystal-cold air, trying to put aside the interview in her brother's chamber.

"Georgina!"

Spinning around, sending swirls of snow everywhere, she discovered Jason coming toward her from the house.

She stood staring at him, her navy blue cape framing her delicate beauty in the whiteness of the world around her. Had he come to berate her even more?

"Georgina, I wish to apologize. I had no right to express an opinion about your family's affairs."

She nodded and turned to go.

"Have you nothing to say?"

"No."

To her surprise, he fell into step beside her. "Where are you going?"

"For a walk."

"With the dog?"

"Chester needs the exercise," she said calmly.

Jason looked at his namesake, struggling through the

snowdrifts. "He will certainly receive exercise trying to wade through such deep snow. Are you not afraid he will disappear in a drift never to be seen again?"

Georgina could not hold back a grin at the humorous look he sent her, but she demanded penance for his earlier behavior. "Would you please carry him as far as the trees? The snow is not as deep there, and he can play."

"Carry the dog?" Jason repeated in disbelief.

"Yes, please."

With a dubious look, first at his elegant cape and then the rather large dog struggling in the snow, he reluctantly nodded. He stooped down and gathered the animal to his chest.

Georgina swallowed her laughter and led the way down the hill to the stand of trees. Once they reached them, Jason set the animal down with a relieved sigh. Georgina helped him brush the snow from his chest.

"You were laughing at me," he accused, seeing the smile on her face.

"Well, you were rather comical, clutching Chester. But I truly appreciate your assistance."

He growled at her but said nothing. Spying boulders a few steps further on, he led Georgina there and swept the snow from one of the rocks. "Your seat, my lady."

"Thank you, kind sir."

After seating himself beside her, Jason picked up a handful of snow and molded it into a perfectly round ball. He hurled it at a nearby tree trunk, hitting it dead center. "Have you forgiven me?"

Georgina, having watched him, now did exactly the same, hitting her target also. "Of course. But I do not understand why you became angry."

"That one over there," Jason said, pointing out a large tree a few yards from their perch. His snowball hit the tree but was slightly off center. Georgina prepared her weapon and launched it at the same target. She hit it several feet lower than Jason and on the opposite side.

"In London, trapping a husband is the latest sport," he assured her as he continued to mold balls of snow.

"But we did not exactly trap Papa. All we did was make it possible for him to get to know Anne better."

"With the express purpose of marriage," he replied, launching another ball at an uncomplaining tree.

"Are you so against marriage, then?"

"No, of course not. But I do not think a man should be pressured into it."

"Do you intend to marry?" Georgina asked, her eyes on his hands as they molded another snowball.

"I suppose . . . someday. I do not see any reason to rush into it."

"I see."

Jason lowered his arm just as he was about to throw another snowball. "I suppose you want to marry?"

"Why do you speak so, as if to marry were to commit some horrible sin? Nathaniel seems perfectly happy to marry Tabitha."

"Because he is receiving the Buxton estate in exchange for losing his freedom."

Georgina pressed her lips firmly together and threw another missile at a nearby tree. She could feel Jason's eyes upon her, but she refused to look his way.

"It is the way of the world, Georgina, and not an insult to your friend."

His words made her turn round; she stared at him with cold eyes. "If the only value I have to my husband is the riches I bring to his coffers, I had rather die a spinster."

"I did not mean that your brother has no appreciation of Tabitha. She is a charming young lady. But neither of us came here with a desire to marry. In fact, we arrived with the specific object of avoiding marriage schemes.''

''At least you are safe, Lord Chesterton,'' Georgina said coolly.

''But I have lost another friend to marriage. I suppose I should be grateful that this marriage is of his own choosing and not a scheme thought up by his sister.'' When Jason turned to look at the young woman beside him, his glance sharpened. ''You did not arrange this marriage also, did you?''

''Don't be ridiculous. You know the whole story.''

''Then why do you look so guilty?''

Georgina Denbigh was raised an honest child. It never occurred to her to lie now. ''Because I had already decided to promote such a match, once Papa was settled.''

Jason sprang to his feet, staring down at her accusingly. ''I cannot believe it! How could you consider such a thing? And I suppose I was next on your list? Do you have another friend waiting to be paired with me?''

Anger got the better of wisdom and Georgina spat back. ''No, I would not offer such a miserable excuse for a husband to my worst enemy, much less a friend!''

Without another word, Jason leaped to his feet and charged up the hill through the heavy drifts of snow, leaving a forlorn Georgina sitting on the boulder with an unused snowball in her hand.

———

When Jason entered the parlor after changing his clothes, he fully expected to find Georgina there. After all, it was already growing dark outside. To his dismay, he discovered only Tabitha and Nathaniel sitting cozily before the fire.

''Where is Georgie?'' he demanded abruptly.

Nathaniel looked at his friend in surprise. "What, Jason?"

"Where is Georgina?" Jason repeated. "Have you seen her, Tabitha?"

"No, not since luncheon."

Jason did an abrupt about-face and returned to the hall. "Wilkins?" he called.

The impassive butler appeared from his pantry. "Yes, my lord?"

"Has Miss Georgina returned from her walk?"

Wilkins frowned in puzzlement. "Did she not accompany you, my lord?"

His cheeks flushed, Jason said, "Yes, but—but I returned earlier than her. Is she above stairs?"

Wilkins's face showed his feelings about Quality's behavior, but he said, "I'll send for Molly, Miss Georgie's maid, my lord."

Jason paced the hall, waiting for Wilkins to return. He occasionally stepped over to the windows by the large front door and stared outside. The snow had increased recently and the sun had already disappeared. In another half hour it would be dark.

"She has not returned, my lord," Wilkins said, his voice expressing the concern his words did not.

"Damn! Wilkins, send to the stables. Have several horses saddled and some volunteers ready. She must have gone after that damned dog. We must find her before it gets dark." He was already running up the stairway when the butler agreed to do as requested.

After accomplishing his directive, Wilkins returned to the hallway to knock on the library door. When he entered, he repeated Lord Chesterton's orders.

"That's not like Georgie," Mr. Denbigh mused even as he moved to follow his butler.

"Is there anything I can do?" Anne asked, following them from the room.

"Make sure there is a warming pan in her bed and Cook has some hot broth ready. If she's been outside for any length of time, she will be quite chilled." Mr. Denbigh then raced up the stairs for his riding boots and warm clothing. Anne descended to the kitchen to alert Cook.

───────

"I wonder what Jason was so excited about?" Nathaniel asked lazily, enjoying the contentment he had found.

"Do you suppose he and Georgina had a disagreement?" Tabitha asked as her needle flicked in and out of her stitchery.

"For what reason?"

"I don't know. But sometimes, they seem to get cross with each other."

"Georgie could get cross with a fence post," Nathaniel said with a grin. "She has a temper."

"She never gets cross with me," Tabitha assured him.

"Of course not. You are too sweet, Tabby. When we are married, I shall have to find reasons to fight with you."

"Why would you want to fight with me, Nathaniel?" Tabitha asked, an uneasy look in her eye.

He shrugged. "To keep you from being bored with our marriage, my dear. Placid water needs stirring up occasionally."

"Or perhaps to keep you from being bored?" Tabitha asked, her gaze pinned on him.

Nathaniel shrugged again. "Never fear. I will have my hands full running both estates. There will be no time for boredom."

He returned to his thoughts, but Tabitha's mind went over their conversation time after time. While she was shy, she was not stupid. She was sure her husband-to-be had just given her a hint as to the direction their marriage should take.

She resolved to talk to Anne and Georgina about her conclusions. This marriage was the most important thing in her life. She would do whatever it took to make it a happy one, even fighting with her husband if that was what he wanted.

Anne entered the parlor. "Has there been any word?"

"Word about what?" Nathaniel asked, rising to his feet.

"Your sister. She is outdoors."

Nathaniel and Tabitha both looked out the window to the growing darkness.

"But she will freeze!" Tabitha exclaimed.

"Why?" Nathaniel demanded.

"I don't know," Anne answered. "Wilkins reported that Jason said she was outdoors. They went out for a walk. He returned but Georgie did not."

"He left her outdoors alone?" Tabitha asked in horror.

"Here, now. Jason is no monster. And it's not like Georgie doesn't often go out alone," Nathaniel said, defending his friend.

"Yes, but—" Tabitha began, only to halt as voices were heard in the entry hall. All three rushed to the door in time to see Jason enter with Georgina wrapped in a blanket in his arms. Her father was beside them.

"Georgie? Are you all right?" Tabitha asked as she hurried to her friend's side.

"Of course I am. It's not as if I was lost. I was on my way back, but I admit it was getting c-cold."

"Is her room ready, my dear?" Mr. Denbigh asked Anne.

"Yes, Molly is waiting for her," Anne promised. "I'll accompany her upstairs."

"I'll go with you," Tabitha added, taking Georgina's

arm as Jason allowed her to slide from his arms to the floor.

"Can you walk?" he asked abruptly.

Georgina turned back to give him a cool stare that was undermined by her chattering teeth. "Of course I can. I am not an invalid."

The three men watched the ladies ascend the stairs before repairing to the parlor. "Wilkins, please bring something to warm us," Mr. Denbigh called over his shoulder.

Once inside the parlor, Jason took several paces across the carpet before saying, "I owe you an apology, Mr. Denbigh. I escorted Georgina to the woods and then abandoned her there."

Though he eyed his guest speculatively, Mr. Denbigh only said, "Do not upset yourself, Jason. Georgina knows our woods well and it is not the first time she has ventured out alone."

"But in this weather, it is dangerous."

"True, but at least you sounded the alarm when you realized she had not returned."

"I should not have left her," Jason continued to mutter to himself.

"Why did you?" Nathaniel asked.

"I lost my temper."

"You and Georgie argued?" Mr. Denbigh asked. "About what?"

"I discovered she intended to . . . that is, she was scheming to bring about her brother's marriage as well as yours."

"But she had nothing to do with my engagement," Nathaniel exclaimed.

"I know that. But when I protested her doing so, she became angry and . . . and I know I should have said nothing, Mr. Denbigh. I owe her an apology for my less than gentlemanly behavior.''

"I gather Georgie's response was less than ladylike also," Mr. Denbigh said wryly.

"It does not matter. The entire incident was my fault, and then I abandoned her in the cold."

"Do not flail yourself quite so determinedly, my boy. Women can be trying at times."

"And yet you choose to marry a second time?"

The incredulity in the young man's voice amused Mr. Denbigh. "I said they could be trying, Jason. But there are benefits to offset that failing."

"I suppose so," Jason replied. His dubious tones only widened the smile on Mr. Denbigh's face.

———

"Are you warm enough, Georgie?" Tabitha asked anxiously, bending over her friend.

"Yes, I am thawing out now," Georgina murmured. "I hope they are taking good care of Chester."

"Where is he?"

"In the stables. Papa insisted he be sent there, as if he had done something wrong."

"Well, isn't it his fault that you went so far from the house?"

"Oh, Tabby, Chester cannot be blamed if he chased a rabbit. That is what he is supposed to do," Georgina said with a sleepy chuckle.

"Why did Jason leave you alone?" Anne asked in a quiet voice.

Georgina tensed under the covers, her shivering forgotten. "He wanted to return to the house."

"It seems strange that he would abandon you in such difficult conditions," Anne persisted.

"If you must know, we had an argument. I—I made

him angry and he walked off. I don't think it occurred to him that I wouldn't return at once." Georgina sniffed and drew the covers up over her cheeks.

"You really should try not to argue with him so much, Georgie," Anne said gently. "After all, you are his hostess."

"I know," she replied with a sigh. "I did not intend to." .

Tabitha spoke up timidly. "Georgie, Anne, I wanted to ask you something." The other two looked at her expectantly, and she dropped her gaze to her tightly clenched hands. "Do you think—do you think one can be too cooperative?"

The other two exchanged glances before Anne said, "That depends, Tabitha. It is always good to cooperate, but one must maintain one's principles."

"Even—even between a husband and wife?" Tabitha's voice expressed her amazement at such a thought.

"Particularly between a husband and wife," Georgina said firmly. "Mama used to argue with Papa frequently when he wanted her to do something she did not like."

"I can't imagine your Papa ever doing anything that was not right," Tabitha whispered in wonder.

"Oh, he did not do bad things, but if Mama did not agree with him, she did not hesitate to tell him."

"Didn't it make him angry?"

"Sometimes," Georgina agreed with a chuckle. "But they always made up in the end."

Anne, who had been watching her charge as Georgina responded, reached out to clasp her hand. "What is it, Tabby?"

"Something Nathaniel said made me wonder if he would not be bored with me if—if we do not argue."

Anne and Georgina exchanged another look. Finally,

Anne said, "Dear one, it is not that you should attempt to quarrel with anyone, but if there is something you believe, you should not allow your beliefs to be disregarded."

"But isn't a man supposed to be more knowledgeable than a woman?" Tabitha asked hesitantly.

Georgina snorted in disgust. "Only because they refuse to allow women to be educated. I'm grateful Papa was not like that."

"Men are human beings, Tabby, but they are not gods. You must think for yourself." Anne added a hug to her statement. "Now, let's return downstairs so that Georgie may rest," she said with a warm smile directed at Georgina.

Mr. Denbigh's appearance at the door only hastened their departure. "May I talk to you a moment, daughter?"

"Of course, Papa."

"You are warm enough?" he asked solicitously after the other women had disappeared down the hallway.

"Yes, Papa, and I'm sorry to have alarmed the household."

"That is to be expected with you and your brother, my dear. From the day both of you were born, life has been one series of mishaps," he said with a chuckle.

"Well, I would have made it back all right," Georgina assured her father, "but I will admit I was glad to be rescued. Chester was very heavy."

"Yes, that dog has a lot to answer for," he grumbled before clearing his throat. "Jason has apologized to me for abandoning you in the woods."

"Oh."

He looked at his only daughter. "I believe you can be a fair trial to some people, my dear."

"I don't intend to be, Papa, truly. Only—well . . . ."

Mr. Denbigh sighed and pushed back the auburn hair so like his own from her forehead. "When you look at me like that, with your most angelic expression, I forget the times I've seen you tease your brother to within an inch of his patience. I suggest you use that look when Jason offers you his apologies."

"Must he?"

"I feel sure he will insist. Of course, it might go more smoothly if you apologized for provoking him."

Georgina's cheeks flooded with color and her eyes fell from her father's face. "Yes, Papa."

"And do not be so hard on Jason. He is too young yet to appreciate women."

"He told you why we quarreled?" Georgina asked with a gasp.

"No, my dear, but I am a wise old man. Just be patient with him."

"Yes, Papa."

# Chapter Twelve

Georgina dreaded going down to breakfast the next morning, reluctant to face Jason after their contretemps. She dressed in her favorite green wool dress and had Molly thread a matching ribbon through her auburn curls. Adding a silk shawl in bright colors gave her confidence, and she marched to the stairs as if she were in a tumbril about to face Madame la Guillotine. To her surprise, only Anne and Tabitha were at the table.

"Where is everyone?" she asked at once.

Anne raised her eyebrows. "And to think I once considered myself to be a person."

"Oh, Anne, I did not mean—you are teasing me!" Georgina took a plate and filled it at the sideboard.

"You are feeling no ill effects from your walk yesterday?" Tabitha asked.

"No, I'm fine. Have the men not come down yet?"

"Ah, that must be who she meant by everyone," Anne whispered loudly to Tabitha.

Tabitha giggled at Anne's teasing and even Georgina smiled. "Of course that is who I meant. I was surprised to discover only the distaff side of our party at table."

"The men have already eaten. They've gone to the stables to see if the sleigh is suitable for use."

"The sleigh? Oh, what fun! I had forgotten about it. Are we going for a ride?"

"Tabitha and I are returning to Mr. Twickenham's residence," Anne said. "We thought it would be nice to have a change of clothing to call our own. Besides, there is a lot to do before the weddings."

"But you will return, won't you?" Georgina asked, a frown on her face.

"I think not," Anne said gently. "I must give your father time to reconsider. I don't want him to accuse me of rushing him into this marriage. And Tabitha and I must pack our belongings."

"Are you going to leave that house vacant?" Georgina asked, struck by the idea.

The other two women seemed startled. Finally, Tabitha said, "I hadn't thought of it, Georgie. I was thinking of it as my father's house, but I guess it will be Nathaniel's after our marriage."

"If you and Nathaniel lived there, and Papa and Anne here, then each of you would have your own establishment and yet still be close enough to visit often. And the servants there are used to your ways," Georgina suggested, thinking aloud.

"That is a very good idea, Georgie," Tabitha enthused. "Don't you think so, Anne?"

"Perhaps. We will need to discuss it with Alistair and Nathaniel, of course. Would you be happy with that arrangement, Tabby?"

"Yes, I think—"

"The sleigh will be ready in half an hour," Nathaniel said as he entered the breakfast room, ushering in a rush of cold air. He was followed by Mr. Denbigh and Jason.

When none of the three ladies responded to his statement, Nathaniel looked at Tabitha. "Aren't you pleased that the sleigh is available?"

"Yes, of course, Nathaniel. We were just discussing our living arrangements after the wedding."

Mr. Denbigh set a cup of hot tea in front of his son, who had taken the chair opposite his fiancée and Jason, before sitting down beside Anne with his own cup. "What arrangements?" he asked.

Georgina studiously ignored Jason, who took the chair next to her. "We just realized that Mr. Twickenham's house will belong to Nathaniel after the marriage, and it seemed appropriate for Nathaniel and Tabby to live there."

"Don't be absurd! This is my home!" Nathaniel cried. The three women exchanged glances but remained silent. Mr. Denbigh pursed his lips in thought. "There is nothing more to be said," Nathaniel affirmed, looking at Tabitha. "We will live here, in my home."

The old Tabitha would have meekly ducked her head and said nothing more to disturb the peace. But the new Tabitha, Nathaniel's fiancée, a young woman whose world had been enlarged by her friendships with Anne and Georgina, looked Nathaniel in the eye. "May I speak to you privately, Nathaniel?" she asked sweetly.

Anne nodded unobtrusively when Tabitha looked her way. Nathaniel, sitting with his mouth agape, suddenly discovered himself the cynosure of all eyes. With irritation, he shoved his chair back and strode from the room, prepared to define their relationship to his future wife.

"A most interesting idea," Mr. Denbigh said with a smile.

"It was Georgina's, actually, but Tabitha thought it a good one," Anne said.

"I have heard that most married couples need time alone without the interference of relatives, and while I must live here, I promise not to bother the two of you,'' Georgina said.

"You show great wisdom, my child. I only hope your brother is as wise,'' Mr. Denbigh said, but his expression did not hold out much hope.

———

"Tabitha! I will not have you contradicting my orders. That must be understood at once.'' Nathaniel glared at the demure young lady sitting composedly on the sofa.

"But I did not, Nathaniel,'' she assured him, her voice wobbling only slightly. She had difficulty maintaining her composure in the face of shouting.

"You might as well have. Everyone knows that you asked to speak with me to change my mind.''

"But, Nathaniel, I only wanted to discuss it with you. How was I to do so unless I asked?'' She looked up at him with her blue eyes wide, framed by dark lashes, and he wondered why he had never noticed how beautiful they were.

He shook his head and looked away. "Now, listen to me, Tabitha. It is a wife's place to do as she is told. I make the decisions because I am the man.''

"Anne says men are not gods.''

"What?'' Nathaniel roared.

"Anne says—''

"I heard you!''

"Then why did you—''

"I do not want you to listen to that woman ever again. I cannot believe my father is going to marry her!''

Shocked, Tabitha rose to her feet. "You—you do not like Anne?''

"I don't mind her, as a general rule, but I have no desire to see her marry into my family. She is a soldier's wife, penniless with no family! My father is too old to marry. The whole idea is ridiculous!''

Standing up for what she wanted was new to Tabby, but she had no doubts at all about standing up for Anne. ''Anne is my friend and I will not hear you speak ill of her!''

Nathaniel whirled around from his contemplation of the fire. ''You will not what?''

''I will not hear you speak ill of Anne. She is a wonderful person, and—and your father is fortunate to be marrying her!''

''You are my wife and you will not tell me what I can and cannot say!'' Nathaniel yelled, overcome by such an unexpected uprising from his demure fiancée.

''I am not your wife yet and—and I will not be your wife if you are going to shout at me! I cannot bear it when you shout at m-me!'' Tabatha cried as she ran from the room.

Nathaniel stood stock still in the center of the room. He felt like a monster. And Tabitha said she would not marry him. Surely she only said it in a fit of anger. She would change her mind later . . . wouldn't she?

Distraught, he rushed back into the breakfast room. ''Papa, Jason, I . . .''

Four pairs of eyes staring at him brought him to a halt. He cleared his throat and stood there awkwardly. He didn't want to admit in front of the other women to the debacle he had just created.

''Where is Tabitha?'' Anne asked.

''Uh, I believe she returned to her bedchamber.'' His voice was husky and he avoided her eyes.

Anne looked at Georgina and rose from her chair, asking to be excused. Georgina followed suit, and soon only gentlemen remained in the breakfast room.

"Sit down and have another cup of tea, son," Mr. Denbigh said, a small smile on his face.

Nathaniel followed his father's suggestion. He kept trying to think how to broach his subject of dealing with a wife when Jason said, "Did your discussion not go well?"

As if the cork had been removed from the champagne bottle, Nathaniel's tale of woe burst forth. "I don't know what happened. One moment I am explaining what she should do, and the next she is running from the room crying! I felt the veriest boor! But I only said . . . that is, I wanted her to . . . Papa! What shall I do?"

"Women are delicate creatures, Nathaniel, and we, as their husbands, promise to care for them and make them happy."

"Well, of course I will make Tabitha happy, but—but she mustn't cry!"

Mr. Denbigh's grin grew larger. "Nathaniel, did you ask Tabitha what she would like to do?"

The young man frowned first at his father and then at Jason. "Why should I ask her? I am supposed to make the decisions."

"Surely, sir, you do not want your son tied to his wife's petticoats?" Jason asked, a little surprised.

Mr. Denbigh shook his head. "Gentlemen, I am going to impart to you some wisdom that will make your marriages happy, if you will only heed my words."

Both gentlemen looked wary but appeared willing to listen. "Though men have always received more education, many women are intelligent and wise. If you respect your wife, and ask her opinion, she will be happy to let you make the decision. At least that has been my experience."

"Ask her opinion?" Nathaniel asked in horror. "Surely you jest, Papa! Why, that is unheard of!"

Mr. Denbigh said nothing, only smiling at his son. Jason sat silently before finally saying, "I have not seen this in any of my friends' marriages."

"And have they been happy in their marriages?"

"No," Jason said thoughtfully. "No, I do not have a single friend who is happy in his marriage."

"No one can promise a happy marriage, Jason, but my first wife was a wise woman from whom I learned much. I expect to learn even more from Anne. That does not mean I was not master in my own home, as I believe my son will attest."

"But what if she does not want what I want?" Nathaniel demanded abruptly.

"Then you each discuss your reasons. If, after listening carefully to her reasons, you have explained yours and neither of you are in agreement, then you must make your decision."

"But Tabitha will cry," Nathaniel warned.

"Perhaps you will change your mind after you hear her reasons," Mr. Denbigh suggested mildly, "and then she would not cry."

"I am sure I am right."

"Then you must learn to deal with tears, Nathaniel," Mr. Denbigh said with a sigh.

———

"Tabitha? Are you all right?" Anne asked as she and Georgina entered the room. The crumpled figure on the bed gave no indication that she had heard the question.

"Was Nathaniel horrible?" Georgina asked. "He can be a bear when he is upset."

There was a quick shake of the silver curls, but Tabitha didn't raise her head. Anne sat down on the bed and pulled the young woman into her arms. "My love, you mustn't cry so. It will make your eyes red."

"I do not care!" Tabitha sobbed into Anne's neck. "We must go home at once, Anne."

"Of course, my dear, just as we had planned."

"No, no, you don't understand! I am not going to marry Nathaniel! I told him I would not marry him," she cried, burying her face again.

There was shocked silence as the other two women stared at her. "But you love him!" Georgina finally exclaimed.

"Yes, but I will not let him say that! I don't care!"

"Say what?" Anne demanded.

"That he—no! I cannot tell you."

"Why not?" Georgina asked. "Was he terribly cruel?"

"No, it is not that," Tabitha said, sitting up away from Anne. "But it was about Anne."

"You argued over me?" Anne gasped.

Tabitha's cheeks flamed. Georgina rushed to her rescue. "I'm afraid my brother is not happy about Papa remarrying."

"I know," Anne assured them composedly.

"You know? Are you still going to marry Papa?" Georgina demanded.

"Yes. Your father assured me he still intended to marry me, no matter what your brother thought." She looked at Georgina. "I did offer to withdraw, but Alistair would not allow it."

"Good for Papa! Nathaniel is being selfish and pompous. You must just ignore him."

"That I can do, but what about Tabby?"

"Do you still want to marry that obnoxious man who is my brother, Tabby?" Georgina asked gently.

"Yes! Oh, yes, I do, Georgie. He does not mean to be so difficult, I am sure, but . . . but he upset me. He shouted at me!" Tabitha dissolved into sobs once more.

Anne took Tabby back into her arms. Georgina looked at the two of them and made up her mind. "I will go talk to Papa and Nathaniel. Do not worry, Tabby. Everything will turn out all right."

There was no one in the breakfast room when Georgina entered. Back out into the hall, she spied Wilkins.

"Where did the gentlemen go?"

"The master and your brother went outdoors, but Lord Chesterton is in the parlor."

Georgina debated her choices, but since she was not dressed for the cold, she chose the parlor. Slipping into the room, she stared at the man leaning on the mantel in deep thought.

"Where did Papa and Nathaniel go?" she finally asked.

Jason whirled around, almost oversetting himself. "Georgie! I—uh, I believe they went to the stables."

"I believe I will join them. Excuse me."

"Shall I accompany you?" He paused before adding, "I promise not to leave you in the cold this time."

His oblique reference to the previous day reminded her of her father's recommendation.

"Georgina? I do apologize for having done so," Jason said, approaching her. "Will you forgive me?"

"Of course, I forgive you," she said. "That is—it is I who should apologize. I should not have said—"

"I am the adult, Georgie. I provoked your anger." His gentleness did not soothe Georgina.

"As you are doing now," she protested, turning away in exasperation. "I am *not* a child. Just because you went away and never returned—" She paused, hoping he would not notice her anguish. "Just because I have not seen you in years does not mean I have not grown up. I am eighteen now!"

Jason drew nearer to her. "I intended to come visit you

sooner," he said, "but the war left us . . . I don't know. Confused, perhaps." He sighed deeply. "It almost made me feel guilty to have survived."

Georgina turned to find him beside her, and one of her hands flew up to caress his cheek. "Oh, no! You mustn't say that, Jason. I prayed so hard each night that you and Nathaniel would be unharmed."

His hand covered hers as he pressed a kiss against her palm. "Do you think those other women left behind were not also praying? I saw better men than me fall to their deaths. But I survived without a mark."

"And I am grateful for God's wisdom," she whispered, her heart in her eyes.

"I have wondered . . ." Jason murmured, his eyes trained on Georgina's soft lips. His voice trailed off as he lowered his head.

When his lips caressed hers, Georgina lost all sense of time and place. Never had she experienced such bliss.

Jason drew back, a look of panic on his face. "I am sorry, Georgie! I should never have . . ."

The euphoria Georgina was experiencing was rudely shattered by his apology. With a cry, she ran from the parlor, pulling the door closed behind her. Not stopping until she reached her room, she sank onto her bed, holding her hands against her hot cheeks.

Now Georgina understood many things. Her beloved Jason, the giant who had befriended a little girl so long ago, was the root of her problem. That magical summer Georgina had given her heart to the young man Jason had been. And though she might deny it, he still possessed her love, however little interest he had in it.

But at least she understood now why no young man she met had touched her heart. That had already been given away by a child to a young man off to war. Unconsciously she had compared each of the green young men she met to Jason, and each had come up wanting.

It made no difference, she thought wearily. With his apology, Jason had clearly shown he had no true feelings toward her. What was it he had said at the pond? Sometimes a man could not resist temptation.

She had waited faithfully since she was eight for his return, but her patience had no meaning to Jason. Because she had been a child when he left, he still considered her a child. Tears ran unbidden down her cheeks as she realized how cruel life could be. That Jason would be spared and yet still be beyond her reach was cruelty indeed. With a sob, she buried her face in her pillow.

# Chapter Thirteen

A solitary figure wrapped in a cloak slid through the stable door and closed it shut against the cold wind. The gloomy day outside left almost no light in the stable. Moving down the row of stalls, the newcomer made little noise. Stopped by the sound of voices coming from a stall further along, where light from a lantern shone through the opening, she listened.

"Mr. Denbigh, I—I have abused your hospitality."

"What are you talking about, Jason? You know we are delighted you are visiting us."

"Yes, but today I—I kissed Georgie." There was anguish in the voice, but the listener showed no appreciation for the emotion.

Silence met his words and Georgie wished she could see their faces. Finally, her father's voice broke the building tension. "Why?"

"I didn't intend to, but we were discussing—that is, I apologized for yesterday and—I don't know."

"How did she react?" her father's calm voice asked.

"She ran away."

"You should not have done that, Jason. I have only kissed Tabitha once, and we are engaged." She recognized her brother's voice. He should tend to his own problems. He had enough of them even if he didn't realize it.

There was a cough, she thought from her father, but it almost sounded like a laugh. What could be humorous? She eased forward trying to see, but it was impossible without revealing herself.

"I know I shouldn't have done so!" Jason's penitent air seemed to have disappeared.

"Have you any intentions toward my daughter?"

She died of shame, that her father should ask such a question! Clearly he did not, or he would have stated them.

"I am willing to marry Georgina, sir. I must marry eventually, and Georgie . . . that is, she will make a fine wife when she matures."

A fine wife? Damned with faint praise!

"Then you have no special feelings for her?"

*Oh, Papa, please! Refuse him and end this tormenting conversation.*

"I—that is, I have always had a warm regard for Georgie. When I spent that summer here—"

"She was eight years old, Jason. Is your feeling for her now the same as it was then?"

"Why, of course! She is older, but—"

"Thank you for the honor you do her, Jason, but I must decline on her behalf."

The listener unclenched her hands even as a tear slid from the corner of her eye to wend its way down her cheek.

"What? Why?"

"Because I want more for my daughter than a forced marriage because of an errant kiss. There are any number of men here in the county who would willingly marry Georgina with more ardor than you have shown. I have not encouraged any of them because I want her to have a happy marriage, a marriage based on mutual respect and love."

"I respect Georgina!" There was a fierceness in his words that surprised her.

"I'm glad, but do you love her? That is an essential ingredient to any good marriage."

"You say that? A man of the world?" The confusion evident in his voice seemed to amuse Mr. Denbigh.

"Yes, Jason, and I would say as much to my son, were it not too late. Though, Nathaniel, I think you would do well to court Tabitha even now."

"Court her? I am already engaged to her!" Nathaniel exclaimed in bewilderment.

"I can see my words have fallen on deaf ears. Thank you for your offer, Jason, but we will just forget the incident occurred."

She pressed back against the wall of the stall, hoping the shadows would cover her presence while her father passed by.

"Do you think he is right?" Nathaniel's voice filled the dark silence.

"About what?" Jason sounded distracted.

"About courting Tabitha. I'm not sure I understand the necessity."

"I don't know."

"I guess you are relieved that Papa refused your offer, though, of course, it was the honorable thing to do," Nathaniel said.

Georgina could not listen anymore. She already knew Jason's feelings on that subject. Pulling her cape close around her, she fled the stables to the snowy world outside. Even freezing was better than being further hurt by Jason's rejection.

———

Georgina sought out Anne as soon as she returned to the house. "Anne, I was unable to speak to Papa because . . .

anyway, could you do so? I believe he just returned to the library.''

Though she looked at the younger woman closely, Anne could see no explanation for the tremor in her voice, but she agreed. ''I'll go speak to him at once. Tabitha is adamant that the engagement is finished. I hope your brother does not feel the same way. That would be disastrous.''

''I don't think he does.''

Anne gave the unhappy Georgina a hug before hurrying down to the library.

''Alistair? Oh, good, you are here. May I speak with you a moment?''

Mr. Denbigh rose from his desk and met his fiancée with his arms extended. She willingly embraced him but wondered if whatever was disturbing Georgie had also affected her father.

''Always, my dear,'' he murmured into her hair.

''Always, what?''

He chuckled. ''Have you forgotten your question so soon? I didn't realize I distracted you so much.''

She leaned back in his arms with a smile on her face. ''Alistair, marriage to you is going to be such a joy.''

''I'm glad you are looking forward to it. I only wish Tabitha and Nathaniel felt the same way.''

''So you know?'' she asked, taking him by the hand and leading him over to the sofa.

Mr. Denbigh frowned. ''I know that their proposed marriage is not a love match. Is that what you mean?''

''No,'' Anne said with a sigh. ''I mean that Tabitha says the engagement is at an end.''

''What? Has she informed my son? Only a few minutes ago he indicated they were still engaged.''

Anne leaned her head against his shoulder. ''I believe

she told him as she ran from the parlor. He probably did not believe her.''

His arm curved around her shoulders, pulling her closer to him. "Ah, the foolish young. They waste so much time and energy on ridiculous fights. Do you know Nathaniel boasted to Jason that he had only kissed Tabitha once, even though they were engaged? He felt he has behaved very properly.''

"I am glad you are not so proper as your son," Anne said demurely, a smile on her face. Mr. Denbigh promptly demonstrated his lack of proper behavior.

A breathless Anne finally asked, "What are we to do about Tabitha and Nathaniel?''

Mr. Denbigh rubbed his chin against her hair. "I think we should let Nathaniel deal with his difficulties. Just because he is my son does not mean I must find the remedy.''

"But what if they do not—I must return with Tabitha to Mr. Twickenham's house.''

Mr. Denbigh pulled away from Anne. "My darling girl, you will be marrying me as soon as the special license has been procured, whether Tabitha and Nathaniel do so or not. After all, according to Jason, I have compromised you just by kissing you. You are obligated to marry me!'' He pulled her tightly against him once more, and the pair shut out the world's problems for a while.

═══════

When the two men returned to the house, Wilkins informed Nathaniel that his father wished to speak with him. He went to the library at once.

"Papa, you wanted to see me?''

"Yes, Nathaniel. You neglected to inform me that your engagement was at an end.''

"What are you talking about?''

"It appears that Tabitha broke your engagement when you had an argument about my fiancée."

Nathaniel's cheeks flooded with color and he dropped his eyes. There was a coolness in his father's voice that informed him he was displeased. "I didn't mean—Mrs. Hansen is a pleasant woman, but—Mama has only been dead a short while."

"Your mother has been dead four years, and I love her today as much as I loved her then. My marrying Anne does not change my love for your mother. But I also love Anne, and I look forward to having a companion again. Would you deny me that?"

Despite his long absence, Nathaniel loved his father and could never have denied him anything presented in such a light. "Of course not, Papa. I guess I did not think."

Mr. Denbigh moved from around his desk and hugged his son. "Thank you, Nathaniel. I told Anne you would not fail me."

"She knows?" Nathaniel asked, horror-stricken.

"She knew before Tabitha told her. Your response has been visible," Mr. Denbigh said dryly.

"I am sorry, Papa. I will apologize to Mrs. Hansen—"

"I believe you should call her Anne since she is to be your step-mama," Mr. Denbigh inserted smoothly.

"Yes, yes, of course."

"Thank you, Nathaniel. I appreciate that. However, it still does not resolve your difficulty with Tabitha." Mr. Denbigh waited for his son's response.

"But Mrs.—Anne will tell Tabitha that I withdraw my objections to your marriage and that will solve everything."

Mr. Denbigh sighed. Nathaniel was a good son, but he had much to learn about women.

"Why are you smiling, Papa? What is wrong with that?"

"I am afraid the resolution will not be so simple. I believe you must talk to Tabitha yourself." Mr. Denbigh opened the library door. "I wish you success, Nathaniel."

"But, Papa, I'm not sure—"

"Go talk to Tabitha. And remember what I said about courting her."

Before Nathaniel knew what was happening, he found himself in the hallway, a closed door behind him. He turned toward the parlor, his steps slow. Surprisingly enough, he discovered he wanted to marry Tabitha. He had grown . . . comfortable with the idea, he assured himself.

He stood poised outside the door of the parlor, gathering his thoughts, when he heard a step on the stairs behind him. When he saw Jason coming down, he breathed a sigh of relief.

"Jason! Just the man I need."

"Really? We only parted a half hour ago. What is it?" he asked casually, adjusting the cuffs of his shirt sleeve under the bottle green coat he had just put on.

"Papa says Tabitha has broken off our engagement and I must convince her not to do so."

Jason's eyebrows rose. "What is the matter? I thought both of you happy with the arrangement."

"It is complicated, but I am prepared to be reasonable about what has upset her. So I see no difficulty, but Papa made a riddle about how I should discuss the difficulty with Tabitha."

"And what am I to do?"

"I thought you would help me talk to her," Nathaniel burst out.

Jason's eyebrows rose again. "Don't you think that might be better done in private?"

Nathaniel clutched Jason's sleeve, as if afraid he would abandon him. "I need you to help me."

As his friend drew him toward the parlor, Jason wondered if he were wise to accompany him. But it appeared he had no choice unless he wanted an argument with Nathaniel.

Once the pair entered the parlor, Jason realized he had another difficulty. Not only was Tabitha in the parlor, but also Georgina, doing her interminable knitting. He called himself all kinds of a coward, but he did not want to face that young lady.

"Tabitha," Nathaniel called loudly, retaining his death grip on Jason. "I would like to speak with you."

Georgina, aware of Jason's presence beside her brother, was eager to depart, but when she moved to rise from the sofa, her friend clutched her arm and pleaded with her eyes not to be deserted. Georgina sat back down and concentrated on her knitting, hoping desperately no one would speak to her.

Nathaniel waited for some response from Tabitha to guide him, but she sat with her hands folded in her lap, her eyes down. Finally, he burst out, "Papa said you considered our engagement at an end."

Even that abrupt opening produced no response.

"Is it true?" he demanded.

"Yes." Her voice was uncharacteristically calm, causing Georgina to look at her in wonder.

"If I apologize for my remarks about Mrs. Hansen and my father's marriage, will you renew our engagement?"

"No."

Nathaniel looked helplessly at his friend, and Jason, despite his intention to remain silent, could not resist his appeal. He moved forward to take a chair near the end of the sofa where Tabitha was ensconced.

"My dear, I know you would not play fast and loose with Nathaniel's heart. Can you not explain the difficulty?"

"Nathaniel's heart is not involved, my lord."

"I never said it was!" Nathaniel exclaimed belligerently. "I did not mislead you."

"No, sir, you did not. Nor did I mean to infer that you did. However, in your strictures about your father's marriage, I realized our marriage is just as unequal as that of your father and Anne." There was silence before Tabitha added kindly, "Do not worry. I will try to persuade my father to sell you the Buxton estate. He has no desire for it, and I cannot live there now."

"Oh, Tabby," Georgina moaned, dropping her knitting and hugging her friend to her.

Jason shrugged his shoulders at Nathaniel. His friend stared at the pair on the couch as if in a trance. Finally he asked a question that surprised everyone.

"Why are you not crying?"

Tabitha drew back from Georgina and stared up at him. "What?"

"Earlier, when I said those things about Mrs. Hansen, you cried. Why are you not crying now?"

"Because I no longer expect you to have those tender feelings for me that I look for in my future husband." She could not quite meet his eyes and her voice trembled, but there were no tears.

Again, Nathaniel surprised his audience. "Does that mean you once felt those feelings for me?"

"That is not fair, Nathaniel!" Georgina exclaimed.

"Really, you should not, as a gentleman—" Jason began, only to be cut off by his friend.

"Let her answer."

Tabitha slowly raised her eyes to the young man now standing in front of her waiting. Her cheeks flamed bright red, and in spite of herself, her eyes filled with those missing tears, but she didn't let any escape. "Yes," she whispered, "I did once."

In a flash, Nathaniel realized he had carelessly rejected a priceless gift. He fell to one knee in front of the trembling young woman. "Tabitha, I have been a fool. If I promise to cherish you, may we renew our engagement?"

She squared her shoulders and said, "I have already promised to persuade my father to sell you the Buxton estate, Nathaniel. Your proposal is truly not necessary."

His hands grasped her two clutched tightly together. "Yes, it is necessary, Tabitha," he said in a low voice, his eyes burning into hers. "I do not care about the Buxton estate. If I lose you, I will have nothing."

Georgina and Jason stared at the couple, entranced by what was taking place before them.

"You cannot mean it," Tabitha whispered.

"With all my heart, dear Tabitha. I think I have finally found what I was searching for all those years in London."

"Me?" she asked as one tear slid slowly down her pale cheek.

"You. I want a happy marriage, like my father's, and a home and children . . . with you."

"Oh, Nathaniel," Tabitha cried as the tears poured down her cheeks.

Georgina hastily moved as her brother joined Tabitha on the sofa, pulling her into his arms. With the sudden realization that she was intruding on a personal interview, Georgina hurried from the room. She was surprised when her hand on the door was covered by Jason's.

''Sorry. I just realized . . .'' he began, and then stopped as he read the same words in her face.

She allowed him to open the door and pull it closed behind them before she said, ''I know. It was so fascinating I forgot I should not have been there.''

He stared down at her radiant smile and felt pain in his chest. ''I hope they will be very happy.''

''Yes,'' Georgina said, but her smile faded as he continued to stare at her, erasing the happiness her brother's romance had provided. ''I must go upstairs.''

''Wait! Georgina, I must apologize for my behavior this morning,'' he said hoarsely, all the while wishing he could kiss her again. He must be crazy!

The frantic look she shot him did not ease his discomfort. She muttered something and sped on her way up the stairs. He wanted to call her back, to tell her he didn't hear her words, to look into her eyes again, but he knew better. At a safe distance, he followed her up the stairs.

# Chapter Fourteen

Nathaniel and Tabitha's reconciliation filled the entire household with happiness, particularly as Nathaniel demonstrated all the signs of a young man besotted by love. A blushing Tabitha met smiles all round as she strove to believe Nathaniel's protestations of undying love.

"Do you think he truly loves me?" she demanded of Georgina several times.

Each time, her friend assured her Nathaniel seemed sincere. Indeed, he could not take his eyes from his new-found love whenever they were in the same room.

Despite Nathaniel's protests, Anne and Tabitha returned to Mr. Twickenham's house to prepare for their weddings. After a short discussion, Nathaniel agreed with the two women that he and Tabitha should take up residence there after their marriage, allowing each newly wedded couple some degree of privacy.

Using the excuse of familiarizing himself with his future home, he made daily trips to visit Tabitha. He was willingly accompanied by Mr. Denbigh, who wished to see his own fiancée. Their desertion left Jason to his own entertainment, since he didn't feel it would be wise to seek out Georgina's company.

Georgina had the task of preparing the house for the upcoming weddings, as well as continuing preparations for the children's party at Christmas. She supervised intensive cleaning and went over menus several times. It was decided the weddings themselves would be private, but the entire neighborhood would be invited for a celebration afterwards.

The third morning, she was crossing the front hall when Wilkins admitted a small, dapper man.

"Miss Denbigh," the man said with a low bow.

"Oh, Masterson, you have returned. How is your father?"

"He is much improved, miss, and thank you for asking. I have returned to my duties. Lord Chesterton is still here?" he asked.

"Yes, he is still here. Wilkins, will you—"

"No, no, miss. There is no need to disturb Mr. Wilkins. I'll just go upstairs myself," the little man assured the young lady, eager to return to his duties.

The question was settled by the appearance of Jason on the stairs. "Masterson!" he called out joyfully as he saw the new arrival. He ran down the stairs to take the short man by the shoulders. "How are you, man? How is your father?"

The valet stared incomprehensively at his employer. Never had his master been known to take such an interest in his employees. "My lord?"

His valet's reaction seemed to embarrass Jason. "I hope your father is better," he stated in a sedate fashion, removing his hands from his employee.

"Thank you, my lord, he is much improved. I am sorry for being gone so long," Masterson said anxiously.

"It is all right, Masterson. I have suffered," Jason said with a small grin slanted at his female audience, "but it could not be avoided. Come above stairs and I'll introduce you to your replacement."

Masterson said nothing, but his eyes shone with concern. While Lord Chesterton, in the past, had not been particularly warm toward his employees, he paid well and never abused them, as some of the Quality were wont to do.

"Jason," Georgina called urgently as the two men set off up the stairs.

It had been several days since his hostess had addressed him directly. Jason turned around, motioning for Masterson to continue without him.

"Yes, Georgina?"

"I just wondered—that is, what will happen to Albert?"

"Is he not welcome to return to your staff?" Jason asked in surprise.

"Of course he is! Yes, of course, he'll return to our staff. Please excuse my bothering you," she said, as her teeth sank into her bottom lip and she turned from him.

Frowning, Jason descended the few steps he had gone up. "What would you have me do, Georgie? Masterson is my valet. I cannot dismiss him."

With her back to him, Georgina replied, "No, of course not. I was being foolish. It is just that Albert has been so proud of his new job. And—and the extra fee you paid him made a difference to his family." She turned back to face him, pasting a smile on her face. "Never mind. It is no concern of yours. Send Albert to me and I will inform him of his change of status."

"I do not delegate difficult duties. I'll explain the situation to Albert myself." When she said nothing else, he turned and followed his valet up the stairs.

Georgina stood at the bottom of the stairs, watching him disappear. It was all of a piece, she decided mournfully. Albert's loss of prestige, her loss of her heart. Only Albert would recover much more swiftly than she.

Several hours later, Georgina was in the morning room, preparing a list of items yet to be accomplished, when Wilkins rapped on the door and then entered. "Miss Georgina, Albert would like to see you."

Bracing herself, Georgina put on a smile and said, "Yes, of course, Wilkins. Show him in."

That young man came bursting through the door, a look of excitement on his face. Georgina stared at him in surprise.

"Miss! Thank you so much! His lordship said as how it was your idea. Wait until I tell me mum!"

"Albert, what are you talking about?"

"Me staying on with Lord Chesterton! I'm goin' to London, miss! Me mum is going to be so proud!" The young man's enthusiasm seemed to grow as he explained.

"But Albert—didn't Masterson return?" Georgina wondered if she had imagined the valet's appearance.

" 'Course, Miss Georgie. That's why I was so surprised. I 'spected His Lordship to throw me out on me ear. He ain't been too complimentary since I took up working for 'im. But instead, he said you suggested I work for 'im as an assistant to Mr. Masterson. He said Mr. Masterson could really teach me, much better than 'im. And Mr. Masterson agreed!"

Albert sounded even more surprised at Masterson's consent than he did Lord Chesterton's. "I'm very happy for you, Albert. I'm sure you will do well under Masterson's tutelage."

"Yes'm, I'll do me best. His Lordship said as how I could have some time to go tell me mum. Is that all right?"

"Of course it is, if he said so. After all, he is your employer, isn't he?" Georgina said lightly, despite the gathering tears in her eyes.

With a grin, the young man sketched a bow and was out the door, saving Georgina from the disgrace of crying in front of him. How kind of Jason, she thought with a sniff. It was a considerate action she had not expected of him, and all the more precious because of its unexpectedness.

========

The Denbigh men brought word that evening that their fiancées would be returning to Greenbriar Manor the next day to see if they could be of assistance to Georgina. She had no need of their assistance, but she looked forward to their company.

The three Denbighs and Jason were all seated at the breakfast parlor when a note arrived from Anne the next morning. Since the women's arrival was expected at any moment, all were curious about Mr. Denbigh's letter.

He wasted no time informing them. "Mr. Twickenham arrived late last evening. He has obtained the special license and his attorneys have prepared the marriage agreement. He will be accompanying the ladies this morning to go over the particulars with you, Nathaniel."

"Does that mean the weddings will be tomorrow?" Georgina asked, mentally preparing lists of tasks to be accomplished.

"I have not yet received the special license I sent for. But it might be best if your marriage went forward as planned, Nathaniel, and Anne and I marry after Mr. Twickenham's departure."

"Tabitha would be most disappointed, Papa," Nathaniel said with a frown. "She has her heart set on seeing you and Anne marry at the same time."

"The problem is not Tabitha but her father," Jason pointed out to his friend. "To have the two of you safely married before he discovers his second bird has flown the coop might be to everyone's advantage.''

Mr. Denbigh nodded in gratitude for having stated their difficulty so succinctly. Georgina, more practical considerations on her mind, asked, ''So shall I send out the invitations to our neighbors for a celebration tomorrow evening? There is no need to state how many weddings we are celebrating.''

All eyes were on Nathaniel. He reluctantly nodded. ''I do not want to upset Tabitha, but I believe you are right. When they arrive, I'll speak to her alone for a few minutes.''

It was over an hour later before the expected party arrived. Nathaniel spent most of that time pacing the parlor, nervously adjusting his cravat. Georgina sat knitting, but her start at every noise proclaimed her worry.

''Do not be concerned,'' Jason whispered, pausing beside her while his eyes remained on his friend, peering out the front window.

''But what if Mr. Twickenham changes his mind?'' Georgina whispered in return.

''He does not want either his daughter or the Buxton estate, if the truth be told.''

''I know, but—''

''They're here!'' Nathaniel exclaimed. He strode to the parlor door, only to be checked by his sister.

''Nathaniel! You must wait here. Wilkins will announce them.'' She busied herself putting away her knitting, and Jason strolled over to stand beside Nathaniel.

When Wilkins opened the door and announced their guests, Nathaniel held back no longer. Rushing forward, he took Tabitha's hands in his as if they had been parted for more than a fortnnight rather than one day.

Georgina stepped forward to speak to both women and then welcome Mr. Twickenham.

"Would'a been here sooner but for the weather. All the traffic north couldn't leave London. Worst snow storm in years!"

"Yes, it was quite amazing, wasn't it?" Georgina remarked, her nerves tied in knots now that the man had finally arrived. "Wilkins, please tell my father that our guests have arrived," she added before the butler closed the door.

Georgina was grateful as Jason continued the conversation with Mr. Twickenham. Nathaniel and Tabitha were to one side, whispering, and Anne was even more distraught than Georgina. She wondered if there had already been an argument among the Twickenham party before their arrival.

When Mr. Denbigh entered the room, Anne rose to her feet and rushed to his side, causing Mr. Twickenham to stop in mid-sentence. "Here now, what's this?"

"Good morning, Mr. Twickenham," Mr. Denbigh said quietly, tucking Anne's hand in his behind him. "We are pleased to see you have safely returned."

"Some more than others," the man said cryptically, his eyes still pinned on Anne.

"If you will excuse us, I must speak to Tabitha alone," Nathaniel explained as he led his fiancée from the room, leaving no one the opportunity to object.

Mr. Twickenham looked from Anne to the departing couple and back to Anne again. "Is there something amiss?" he questioned, a heavy frown on his brow.

"No, sir," Mr. Denbigh replied. "Nathaniel and Tabitha are eager to wed. You have brought the agreement with you?"

Though he was distracted by Anne's closeness to his

neighbor, Mr. Twickenham produced the agreement and offered it to Mr. Denbigh.

"Also," Mr. Twickenham began, pausing to clear his throat, "I wondered if we might kill two birds with one stone, so to speak."

Everyone in the room except Anne waited expectantly for his next words.

"I thought as how you've made all the preparations for one wedding, we might just as well have two," he suggested, a beaming smile on his face.

"I told you—" Anne began in an agitated fashion, but Mr. Denbigh silenced her with a caress to her cheek.

"Whose marriage are we talking about?" he asked calmly.

Mr. Twickenham's eyes were glued to the pair as he said, "I bought a special license for me and Mrs. Hansen, also. I believe I told you we were to be married."

"You stated your intention to marry Mrs. Hansen. As I recall, she refused your proposal.

" 'Tis no matter. She'll wed me, right enough. She's just being coy." His bluff assurance brought a flush of angry red to Anne's cheeks.

Mr. Denbigh pulled Anne's hand from behind his back to join his other hand in front. "I'm afraid you are wrong, Mr. Twickenham. You see, Anne is going to marry me."

"What?" the man roared, his face red. "How dare you steal my bride from me! There'll be no wedding betwixt our offspring if you do such a thing!"

Anne's cheeks paled, but when she would have protested, Mr. Denbigh whispered something to her. Placing his arm round her, he said quietly, "You must do whatever you think is right, Mr. Twickenham, but Mrs. Hansen and I are to be wed as soon as we have obtained a special license.'' Without waiting for a response, he led his bride-to-be from the room.

Georgina and Jason, left alone with the enraged Mr. Twickenham, exchanged startled looks. Not knowing what to say, Georgina murmured, ''I'll ring for tea.''

''I'll drink no tea in this house! Send for my daughter at once! She'll live her life as a spinster before I'll let her marry the son of that duplicitous man!''

Georgina looked at Jason again. With a nod toward the bell-pull, he placed a hand on Mr. Twickenham's arm. ''I can understand your feelings, Mr. Twickenham. But it will take several minutes to discover the whereabouts of Tabitha. Come, be seated and let Miss Denbigh serve you a hot cup of tea.''

Mr. Twickenham did not resist Jason's escort to one of the sofas, but he sounded no less angry when he said, ''She'd best be found at once. I'll not tolerate being in this house much longer. And as far as that harpy goes—''

Georgina, returning from her talk with Wilkins, gasped at such a remark, but Jason commanded her silence with his eyes.

''Actually, that is what surprised me about your proposal.''

Both Mr. Twickenham and Georgina stared at him in surprise. Finally, Mr. Twickenham said, ''What do you mean, young fellow?''

Jason ignored the absence of his title and leaned forward as if confiding a secret. ''You see, you have the reputation in the city of being such a downy one. That's why I couldn't understand your offering for Mrs. Hansen.''

''Why wouldn't I offer for her? She's attractive enough.''

''Of course, for a woman her age, she is quite attractive. But a man of your stature could choose a young bride, perhaps even quality, and produce a family of sons to carry on in his footsteps.''

"Not sure I want more children. My one chick hasn't brought me a lot of pleasure," Mr. Twickenham growled.

"And then, of course, there's the matter of her family."

"Her family? I understood she was alone in the world!"

Georgina gulped and stared at Jason. What would he say now?

"I suppose it is no *lie* to say that. Not precisely. But her husband's family is multitudinous, and well known for being in the hands of bloodsuckers and cent percenters. I warned Mr. Denbigh of that, but he seemed to think he would be able to escape paying all their bills." Jason shook his head sadly, as if he were sure his host was being foolhardy.

"She never mentioned them," Mr. Twickenham muttered.

"No, and I'll bet you've seen neither hide nor hair of them. They have no use for her now that she's penniless. But when her husband was alive, they dogged their every step."

"But he had no money, just his officer's pay."

"And that was more than they had. Just wait until they hear she might be marrying you," Jason said with enthusiasm, as if he couldn't wait to return to London and pass on such interesting gossip.

"Here, now! No need to spread that about!"

"But it's true, or almost true. I'm sure Mr. Denbigh will not be able to withstand your threat. After all, the Buxton estate is a handsome one. And you can be sure that once the hope of marrying Mr. Denbigh is gone, Mrs. Hansen will not let you escape her net. After all, you proposed in front of witnesses." Jason paused to rub his chin. "In fact, she might take you to court and win a large sum even if you didn't marry her. Breach of promise, I believe it is called.''

''No! No, I won't pay that woman off! She wants to marry Mr. Denbigh! You heard her!'' Mr. Twickenham shouted, rising to his feet. ''I'll call you both as witnesses!''

''Oh, she'll probably marry him if he will agree to it, but he is a devoted father, you know. I doubt he'll take his own happiness at his son's expense.''

''I'll agree to their marriage. I'll even offer a large wedding present—something grand, ten thousand pounds!''

Georgina almost laughed aloud as the man clutched his coattails to his rotund figure, as if he feared Anne might rob his pockets even as he stood there.

''That is most handsome of you, Mr. Twickenham. Perhaps we should add that to the agreement you brought with you. It would convince Mr. Denbigh and his son that you are in earnest,'' Jason suggested genially, as if he had only Mr. Twickenham's best interests at heart.

''Yes, yes, of course. Glad to do so. Do you think Mr. Denbigh will marry her, knowing about her family?'' There was anxiety in his voice, and Georgina and Jason exchanged looks.

''I believe he will do so. Georgina, could you not talk to your father? It would relieve Mr. Twickenham greatly if he could have your father's assurance that he intends to marry Mrs. Hansen.''

''Of course, Jason. But I wondered, if the special license does not already have names on it, if you should offer it to my father. I believe he and Anne could marry tomorrow along with Nathaniel and Tabitha.''

Mr. Twickenham's eyes narrowed. ''Now why would you be willing to help your father into such a trap, missy?''

With great aplomb, Georgina looked sad as she said,

"Because my father believes he truly loves Mrs. Hansen. And it is not Anne's fault she has such terrible relatives."

"That may be true, but I'll not have hungry relatives yapping around my door. I'll gladly give him the special license. I have no use for it." Mr. Twickenham sat back relieved, and Georgina sped through the open door as Wilkins entered with the tea tray.

# Chapter Fifteen

The Denbighs' neighbors were enjoying a bountiful buffet in the dining hall while others were dancing to the music in the ballroom. The chandeliers sparkled and the rooms were festooned with garlands of holly and greenery. Large fires crackled in both ends of the ballroom, drawing guests to their warmth, and servants mingled among the crowd, offering cups of punch from the huge silver wassail bowl her father had again insisted be used, even though it was still several weeks until Christmas.

Mr. Twickenham had been invited to remain for the party, but he chose to make a late start for London, much to everyone's relief. He said he never wanted to set foot in the country again now that he was rid of his property. No one objected.

Jason stood against the wall, surveying the gathering. Mr. Denbigh's contentment, along with his wife's, the former Mrs. Hansen, was visible to all. Tabitha and Nathaniel, the other newlyweds, appeared almost delirious with joy. They scarcely noticed the company surrounding them. Fortunately, everyone was amused by their distraction rather than offended.

The figure that drew Jason's eyes the longest, however, was Georgina. He watched her gracefully sway to the steps in her amber satin gown, her creamy shoulders gleaming almost as much as the material. She was a beauty, no doubt about it.

He looked away. It was time he returned to London. In London there were women, sophisticated women who could make him forget an innocent like Georgina and the inexplicable desires she could evoke. His eyes returned to linger on Georgina. Yes, he must return to London.

He slipped from the room and ran up the staircase. The urgency he felt surprised him, but he supposed he was ready to resume his normal way of life. And there was no time like the present. In his room, he rang the bell and waited impatiently for Masterson to appear.

The servant ran into his room, gasping from the rapid climb up the steep servants' stairs. "Yes, my lord?"

"I'm sorry, Masterson. There was no need to run, but we are departing in the morning. Can you and Albert get everything packed this evening?"

The servant bowed and said, "Of course, my lord. If that is what you wish."

Jason frowned. "Of course, that is what I wish. We have been here too long as it is. Now that the weddings are over, they will be in no mood for entertainment."

"Yes, my lord."

Frowning even more, Jason seemed on the point of saying something else, but he stopped himself, only giving a curt nod, as if he were angry, and left the room.

"Cor, he's in a rare taking," Masterson muttered, even as he began the mammoth undertaking.

———

After more than a week of attempts to dispel his malaise that had gripped him since his return to London, Jason sat at the dinner table, ignoring the dishes presented to him. Unaware that his French chef was threatening suicide if at least one specialty did not tempt his lordship, Jason stared dismally down the long, empty table. He had invited several cronies to dinner to fill those places on other nights, but he had found no pleasure in it. He could not continue as he was. Everyone had noticed his lethargy.

One of his friends, when he thought Jason was not listening, had said, "He acts like a man in love."

He had resisted such a thought. Now he decided to put his suspicions to the test. With great ease, he pictured Georgina sitting at the foot of his table, dressed in her amber satin gown, her lips curved in a smile. There was a leap of his heart that amazed him. He picked up his wine glass and saluted the vision, causing his butler to stare at him.

But Jason ignored everything but the young woman in his mind's eye. He dwelled lovingly over their walk in the snow, and his carrying her back to the house, her shivering body pressed against his. He remembered the kiss he had so rashly given her. The sight of her seated in the hay, holding her mare's head, as Noelle was born, brought a warm smile to his face.

And the deviltry in her eye as she showered him with snowballs brought an answering gleam to his, intensified as he remembered her beneath him in the snow, her body responding to his.

Could it be true? Could Georgina be the answer to his problem? Had he been blind, still thinking of her as a child, the eight-year-old who had so charmed him, his fear of love hiding his true feelings? He had not been able to respond to any of the lures thrown out to him this week from eager women, wanting to fill Marietta's role after he had discovered he had no interest continuing with her. But the thought of Georgina fully clothed stirred him as no mistress ever had.

He picked up a fork and tore into the roast beef the

butler had just started to remove. With a relieved sigh, the servant withdrew and reported to the chef that his lordship approved of the beef.

While eating with more appetite than he had shown since his return, Jason's mind raced along at a fast clip. Did she care for him? After his kiss, she had all but avoided him. He knew she would not accept his proposal if she did not love him.

He put down his fork and stared into space once more. The butler hovered, unsure whether he should remove the plate or not. Finally, he ventured to ask if his lordship was ready for dessert.

Jason stared at him as if he had not seen him before. "What? Oh, yes, I—yes, dessert." He returned to his thoughts. He didn't want to wait to determine his fate. He must return to Greenbriar Manor. He rose from his chair just as the butler entered with his dessert.

"Oh, I'll not need that, Dithers. You may eat it."

The butler stared at him, but his master wandered from the room. Dithers looked down at the dish. The chef would be distraught if it was returned untouched. With a quick dart of his eyes to ensure no one was about, the butler picked up a fork and enjoyed several bites of dessert. After all, his master had ordered him to do so.

———

"Anne, my dear, I'm expecting a visitor today. Would you ensure that a room is prepared?" Mr. Denbigh asked his wife as he enjoyed his breakfast.

"Of course, Alistair," Anne answered calmly. Since she had already been informed by her husband that morning before he left her bed, she showed no surprise.

Georgina looked up. "Who is coming, Papa?"

"An old friend. Are Nathaniel and Tabitha moving to

the Buxton estate next week?'' he asked, in hopes of distracting her.

''They have decided to wait until after the new year, Papa. Though they intend to drive over this afternoon and begin preparation for their move.''

''Hmmm, is all in order for the children's party?''

''Oh, yes. I finished the last of the mittens yesterday. Anne helped me with them,'' she said with a warm smile to her new step mother. ''And—and the sugar candies Jason sent from London will please all the children.''

''Yes, that was most kind of him, wasn't it?'' Mr. Denbigh said with a smile.

''Yes.'' It was kind of Jason to remember the children, Georgina thought, but there had been no message for her. She would not admit to herself how many times she had read the brief note that had accompanied the candies. But no matter how often she read it, the note remained an impersonal thanks for their hospitality. At least it showed his thoughtfulness.

She had worked hard to remove him from her thoughts, but that too had been a failure. She sighed as she stirred her tea.

''What do you have planned for today?'' Anne asked her.

''I thought I might ride over and visit Albert's mother. She misses her son.''

''May I accompany you? We could take her some of Cook's gingerbread and a ham from the pantry.''

''I would love your company, Anne, if Papa can spare you,'' Georgina said.

The happiness of both couples only emphasized Georgina's loneliness, but they were careful to include her in their activities. The two women set out to visit their tenant and Mr. Denbigh returned to his library, a smile on his face.

He had been concerned about his daughter's depression until the letter arrived yesterday from Jason. Its contents had relieved him greatly, if he had diagnosed his daughter's problem accurately.

———

When Georgina and Anne returned to the stables, there was a carriage in the stableyard that the younger woman immediately recognized. After all, she had stared at it long enough as it had departed. "That's Jason's carriage."

"Are you sure?" Anne asked cheerfully.

"Yes! Yes, I'm sure. Why would he have returned?"

Anne shrugged her shoulders, carefully hiding any knowledge in her eyes.

Georgina slid from Dumpling's back without waiting for assistance. "Come, Anne," she urged. "We must see if it is truly Jason."

As soon as they entered the hall, she demanded of Wilkins, "Is that Lord Chesterton's carriage in the stableyard?"

"Yes, Miss Georgie. He's in the library, awaiting your return."

Without a thought to her appearance, Georgina hurried down the hall, assuming Anne would follow. After all, Jason was visiting with her father.

When she opened the door to the library, she discovered Jason alone, standing before the fireplace. "Jason! How nice to see you again," she said, trying to sound like a gracious hostess rather than an eager lover.

He spun around and advanced to take her hands in his. "Thank you, Georgina. It is good to see you again."

"Where is Papa?" Georgina asked, her gaze darting

away from him only to return, devouring him with her eyes.

"I believe he is awaiting us in the parlor." Jason retained his hold on her hands, though he longed to pull her into his arms.

"Shall—shall we join him then?" Georgina asked, confused.

"No, not yet." He led her over to the sofa before he continued. "I must ask you something first."

Georgina starcd into his grey eyes, scarcely aware of his words. She was so grateful just to see him again. "Yes?" she murmured.

"Georgie, when I saw you again after all those years, I thought—my memories of you were of a sweet child. I could not adjust to the change in you."

"One cannot remain a child forever, Jason," Georgina whispered.

"No, no, I realized that. I left for London because I did not understand what was happening to me."

"What do you mean?"

"Georgie, do you feel anything for me? I should not ask that. I want to tell you that I love you!" he said in a rush. "I want to explain things—" He never completed his sentence.

Georgina thought their first kiss disturbing, but the one in which she was now participating filled her with delirious joy. Her arms went round his neck and she felt his encircle her waist, pulling her close against him.

When he removed his lips from hers, Jason bowed his head onto her shoulder. "My love, I hope that means you care for me also, because if it does not, you are a very forward young lady."

Georgina caressed his cheek with tingling lips. "I have

been known to be forward, my lord," she replied demurely, "but never in such a way."

Leaning back to see her beloved features, Jason said, "My Georgina, I hope you save all your forward behavior for me alone." Her melting acceptance of his statement left him distracted for several minutes. Finally, he put her away from him.

"Have you changed your mind?" Georgina asked with a pout, confident she knew his answer.

"Behave yourself, young lady. We are supposed to join your father in the parlor. Before we do so, however, I have something for you." He reached into his coat pocket and produced an old-fashioned diamond and emerald ring. "This is the family betrothal ring. Will you wear it?"

With tears in her eyes, Georgina extended her left hand, nodding mutely. He slid the ring on her finger and then carried it to his lips in salute. "Georgie," he said hoarsely, "I cannot live without you. I returned to town because I thought love was not for me. But I had already fallen in love. Don't ever leave me."

With an exquisite sigh, Georgina melted into his arms again. "I have no desire to live without you, Jason. I have loved you ever since you showed such kindness to me as a child."

Jason frowned and pulled back. "Georgina, I love you as an adult, not a child. You do understand that, don't you?"

With a gentle laugh, Georgina pressed against him. "I think so, Jason, dear. After all, you did not kiss me like that when you went off to war." She emphasized her point with a kiss that drove all doubts from his mind.

As she withdrew, her fingers trailed down his cheek. "You see, I am no longer a child, either."

"No, you are not," Jason agreed with satisfaction. "But I will always treasure my memories of that sweet child."

"Good. But we will create new memories, my love. Perhaps even of another child who will follow you around with wonder one day."

"Another child?" Jason asked absently, his hands and eyes enjoying Georgina.

"One of our own," she whispered as she moved back into his arms. "And we will create the sweetest memories of all."